TALES OF TEXAS: SHORT STORIES

AN ANTHOLOGY OF TEXAS FICTION

brought to you by

Printed in the United States of America

First Edition: August 2017.
ISBN: 978-0-9911435-3-5

Except where noted, interior illustrations by Colleen D'Antoni.
Book design by Megan LaFollett.
Compiled by Elizabeth Domino.

Houston Writers House
http://houstonwritershouse.net/

Foreword

IT IS OUR HONOR to serve as Directors of Houston Writers House. The aim of the organization is to assist, promote, encourage, and to teach our members to saddle up and get on with it.

This bevy of Texas Tales are full of fun details of a state rich in history, fantastical creatures, and a wide variation in topography. It is HWH's first publication under our direction and we are proud as sweet tea punch that our writers are so talented. We know y'all will enjoy each story as much as we did.

So get your spurs on and enjoy the ride!

Denise Ditto Satterfield & Rebecca Nolen

Contents

About the Artist

Colleen D'Antoni was raised for most of her childhood in Longview, Texas. She graduated from Spring Hill High School with numerous honors.

Her college education took place on the east coast, at Savannah College of Art and Design in Savannah, Georgia; where she earned a BFA in Illustration.

Colleen currently lives in Dallas, Texas, and aspires to continue her education in art. Though she considers herself a painter at heart and loves working in oil paint, focusing mainly on portraits; she is well versed in a variety of mediums. Her inspiration comes from various places, people, and situations. She loves spending time outside, walking her dog or cycling, and hopes to one day travel around the world.

Instagram: @c.dantoni
Facebook: C.D'Antoni

Lubbock, TX 2001

By Rebecca Nolen

Lubbock, TX 2001

Sinners of every shade
run with the earnest student body,
sneaking across the county line
to buy drive-thru beer
perhaps in Spanish,
despite drop-dead bar maidens in tank-tops serving in loud
Friday night eateries where I hear
cowboys, stripped of their spurs,
don't clank.

The breeze blows twenty-four seven
except maybe Monday and the
sun sheds, thick as dust, on
fields and fields and fields of cotton.
Crooked trees surround and close against
pebble-roofed houses laid out in a grid
waiting for their turn in the next horror movie.
And where in tarnation does that great
seafood restaurant get its fish?

Windmills spin at the big barn
above the forest where lions roar
when they're lonely, which means
all the time, especially
as tumbleweeds roll
past their cages and the
coyotes circle, laughing at them, but only at 3 AM.
Meanwhile, west cattle yards bleed scent east.
And the prevailing wind rolls south from north.

Dry is the weather talk in between the
floods of fall when the streets are filled again.
And around that time we pray that once again
the Aggies blush Ranger Red, and
for once the Longhorns get stuck.
It's for certain that triple W dot TTU dot EDU
is the best dang site to learn about
the migration patterns of long-tail
butterflies and Norwegian rats.

In the land of Texas Tech the sand and the dust
are just grit to your sandwich,
as 80 MPH currents rip Saltillo tiles off of roofs.
The next morning blood and orange sand mix on the sidewalk,
but too much beer and too much music
drowned the news of who was hurt.
Our dead Buddy Holly sings, as
Aeonian wind moans its changing song
unrequited against bent grass.

Sons and daughters, nieces and neighbors are students who make good
or not, and now best friends are old roommates.
Don't think that though you aren't here,
you ever left.
And in the end,
don't forget our Courtney.
Her memory lies shattered across black ice and the gust-riddled empty plain,
and we – every last one of us – miss her still.

About the Author

Rebecca Nolen grew up in the country just outside Houston's city limits, running after horses, handling snakes and building treehouses in which to read. (Those running fields are now Beltway 8.) Early on she wanted to be three things: a writer, an illustrator, and a famous singer. As she can't carry a tune, she opted for the other two choices and went to art school and later taught herself to write. The best thing she ever did from the beginning was to join a couple of writing organizations and a serious critique group. She has two published novels and a closet full of unpublished manuscripts. She contributed a few of her pen and ink drawings to the anthology, *Tales of Texas: Short Stories.*

Over John's Ashes

Written by Caroline Cao

OVER JOHN'S ASHES

"NAM NO AI YI da fu," Linh Pham hissed with zero serenity, her palms cramping around the cold, scaly rubber of the steering wheel. She pressed so firmly that the pressure upon her pearl wedding band would leave a red, lasting imprint. She gazed ahead at the beams from the lights of speeding vehicles, their lights like dispersed, oversized fireflies. *Oh crowded, unbearable Houston. Oh, Buddha, give me peace, may you squeeze my daughter's voicebox... forgive me.*

As Linh swerved onto Exit 45, her hands shivering on the wheel. Marcie had been twisting the car's A/C knobs to the maximum. Linh couldn't tell if it was out of boredom or to make Linh a Popsicle. The girl had forgotten to charge her iPhone so now she was left salvaging entertainment from the controls, her right hand crushing her hollow Red Bull can in ear-grating metallic creaks.

"Marcie, pipe down, *iam lang*."

In response, Marcie flung the can onto the floor. This would be their first Vietnamese New Year without John, the girls' father.

Every year on a midnight in mid-February, they would go to the Jade Buddha Temple's Dragon Dance, a ritual to purge the world of evil and shower the temple and its attendees with good luck.

Her younger daughter, Quinn liked the puppeteers beneath the slink of the fabric skin and tamers in yellow tunics and grinning porcelain masks flapping their scarlet fans at the Dragon's face, always clapping her hands and flashing her rare toothy smiles at them.

Marcie, not so much—anymore.

John's parents, the girls' Bai Naoi and Ong Naoi, had organized with the monks to place John's photo in the memorial room. Every temple had a memorial room for the deceased so the living might lay apples, oranges, rice, and soy fish upon an altar so the deceased might have snacks in the afterlife ("Better than giving dead Americans flowers to smell in Heaven," Linh had joked). Linh and the girls had yet to see it despite Ann's nagging phone messages.

"Don't pray for me when I'm gone," John had beseeched from the deathbed before his brain cancer claimed his ability to make articulate words. John hated to be a burden, knowing how the temple was fifty minutes away from home and the arduous task of bowing a hundred times while chanting Vietnamese hymns in the haze of incense. The custom was to pray every Sunday for a year after a person's demise. Although Ann was present to hear this request, she still pushed Linh to do the prayers, unwilling to accept that Linh had now started working overtime at the optometry office to compensate for the income that John could no longer provide.

Linh had bribed Marcie with five bucks to skip the re-airing of a basketball game.

Maybe she should have given her five more for silence.

"*Mai uh,*" Marcie sat in the front passenger seat, as stiff as a mall mannequin.

Linh had a hard time making eye contact with Marcie. Not because she was fixing her eyes on the road, but because Marcie had her father's intense stare that flared with a fierceness that made Linh swear that John's ghost possessed her.

Answering her eldest daughter would mean giving in.

"What time is it?" Linh eyed the van in front of her and wondered if that family was also on the way to temple. Her foot lifted from the gas pedal so she wasn't tailgating.

"We need to talk." The fifty-minute drive must have boiled Marcie's blood. If John had been there, Marcie wouldn't dare speak in such a contemptuous tone.

"It's eleven-thirty-two," Quinn called from the backseat. She slumped down like a grim-faced rag doll, her cell phone above her face, her fingers poised as if in the middle of a text.

Linh glanced at the rear-view mirror to see Quinn's ambivalent expression.

Their faces were identical, even down to their short haircuts. For a second, she thought she was seeing double of herself. Quinn was a miniature of her, minus the wrinkles, and she was heavier. Doctors swore she was American average size, and once had to explain to John that Quinn wasn't even close to overweight. When Linh was Quinn's age, she had to squash into an overcrowded dirty boat with a booming motor on its way to the refugee camps where she had to wear oversized sweaters and gowns from donation crates.

Quinn popped cuties into her mouth and fixed her eyes on her phone. Her smiles were as scarce as soap bars in Saigon. Her face bore her default straight-lipped frown. Linh wondered why she hadn't even mustered one expression of sadness at her father's funeral. But maybe that was a positive quality. Linh recalled her mother's, her *mai's,* old adage: Sorrow is seldom expressed well. Sorrow has to be locked in a chest in your mind so it won't weigh you down.

They had plenty of time to reach temple, but she could still picture Ann, her mother-in-law, her gray curls stiffened by hairspray, tapping her foot impatiently at the wooden steps of the temple with her quiet husband, Tom, at her side. If Linh arrived earlier than punctuality itself, she wouldn't be spared from Ann's scolding. But at least they could secure good spots close to the Dragons for their good fortune. Perhaps Ann yakked at Linh because she was the definition of an inadequate Buddhist, someone who attended temple services twice a year rather than weekly. Something John pretty much did too, in his adult life—"I believe in a higher power but my *mai* is as ridiculous as Catholics"— though he received less reproach from his mother.

"Can we talk, *mai uh*?" Marcie rarely used Vietnamese terminology. She wanted something. When Marcie was four, Linh had told her Vietnamese folktales, and sung the Vietnamese songs, such as the story about the cat that climbed the tree to find the mouse, to school her in her native language. Marcie had sung the songs sometimes but stammered on her Vietnamese, as Linh had mumbled her English in American high school. Linh lost patience with teaching Marcie. As a result, she had not bothered teaching Quinn, and decided she could live with her future grandchildren not speaking their heritage language.

Bzzzzzz. Linh's velvet purse began to vibrate. "Marcie, that's your Ba Naoi, reach into my purse, call her, tell her we're near."

Marcie continued, "I need a car. For college."

Now she was concerned about college?

After Linh slaved over scholarship papers that Marcie barely qualified for? After announcing that she didn't need a GPA to "get a life?"

"I deserve my own car around a campus," the teenager protested. "I take Quinn to her stupid school every day. For nothing too!"

Bzzz. Golly, Ann.

There was a huff from the backseat. Linh could see that Quinn did not even look up from her cell phone nor stop chewing on an orange. Quinn had a knack for multitasking.

Bzzzzzz. If only she found the time to switch her cell phone to silent. Linh nearly forgot to toggle the left-turn signal as she turned into a neighborhood. She flicked it when she was mid-turn and slapped it off within a second after entering Quarter Avenue.

She wanted to tell her teen daughter, *well, pray for a car at temple.* Why did her girl want a car all of a sudden? Weren't colleges made so people could walk around them? During her university years, she had to walk miles to get to class. Didn't Marcie know she was blessed with rubber Nike sneakers to guard the soles of her feet? In her days, Linh had to walk miles on bare feet over jagged roads, sharp as arrow tips, and muddy grass like shallow quick-stand to evade the Communist patrols.

She could see the temple, a rectangle looming over the oaks and one-story homes. She steered into the white dividing strip between the roads. The parking gate appeared... she flicked the left-turn signal. Her fingers tapped the wheel. Now to let traffic pass. So many cars and trucks turning into the parking lot. She would have to pray for a parking space.

"They're yielding for you." Marcie grumbled. Sure enough, two cars on both lanes had stopped. "They're yielding."

Why did Marcie want to prove Linh the inferior driver? To get a car sooner?

"God, they're yielding."

The cars hadn't moved in seconds despite the influx of traffic behind them. Her foot dropped on the pedal.

Metal shattered and churned. There came an earthquake worse than the waves of the sea that might swallow her. Her scream caught in her throat as her seatbelt constricted her chest and flung her into the seat and then forward toward the panel. The smoke bunched at the windows and she could see the front hood popped open. The engine groaned a seething *hiiiissssssss,* like an upset stomach.

A high-pitched bell rang in her eardrums as she pried her hands off the steering wheel. The world had frozen before her. It took the slap of Marcie's hand on her shoulder to back her back to her senses.

When it was clear the car wasn't moving, Linh tried but could not cry out her daughter's names.

There was a cough from the backseat. It was Marcie who screamed, "Quinn, Quinn, are you—"

"What, I'm fine, I'm ok! I was just choking."

Quinn unfolded from a fetal position and orange peels fell from her hands. She must have gagged on the slices.

Linh had not seen Quinn this furious since the time when John reprimanded her for choosing dark blue shirts at Old Navy, accusing her of becoming one of those "black-wearing, wrist-slitting Goths on the television."

"Quinn," Linh's pitch rose as she fumbled to disengage her seatbelt. "Stay here, girls."

Linh stumbled through the engine-stenched smog, almost dropping to the road as the fumes seeped into her nostrils. The cloud parted enough for her to find the front of her silvery-blue Honda crushed into the door of a cream-colored truck. They were inundated by a barrage of infuriated honking. The drivers of the cars who had yielded for her rolled down their windows to holler profanity.

Linh had failed to note the third lane.

Some people walked out of the parking gate at the temple to investigate the source of the commotion, clad in their Sunday best and their stiff-collared *ou dai* frocks. The car lights from the two yielding cars were like an unwelcom spotlight.

Linh ran to the door of the truck and saw the silhouette of the driver at the window, motionless.

Her fingertips lingered at the door handle.

She didn't want to see the carnage.

Linh recoiled when the door was flung open by a hairy arm. An unshaven, bulky man of bodybuilder size, his crucifix necklace sticking to the sweat- soaked gray T-shirt, stepped out, stumbling onto the pavement. Linh took two steps back, overwhelmed by his size. As the man loomed closer, Linh saw his astonished expression when he made eye contact with her. A million apologies would not fix this, so she couldn't bring herself to utter, "I'm sorry." It would have come out pathetically and the smoke in her lungs clung to her voice box. She could only squeal, "I'll pay," as she cringed at the thought of him naming the thousands of damages. No, no, no, she was still contending with bills from John's several surgeries and funeral, especially for that Redwood casket that was cremated with him.

Then a lady emerged from the passenger seat.

Linh recoiled. The lady surveyed Linh like a judgmental English teacher.

"Stupid chink!" The tanned lady spat out, the words curled in a vengeful Latino accent. She wasn't the first to say a schoolyard slur to Linh. Linh was tempted to call the woman a slur herself, but she knew no slurs for Hispanics. For that she was thankful.

"Stupid chink!" And the lady burst into a rapture of garbled Spanish that Linh could only interpret as a reproaching prayer, judging by the recurring sprouts of "Hail Mary." Linh planted her feet firmly on the ground, making resolute eye contact with the woman's glare.

Communist woman. Nice to shout it in her head. *Commie woman. Commie woman, cowardly woman.*

The blinking light of blue and red, like synthetic shades of the American Flag, caught their attention. The two women turned their attention to the police vehicle pulling up to the scene. The woman ran to her husband.

Quinn had settled on the patch of grass below the sidewalk, clutching the candy bag, her eyes on the crash site as if the accident had not happened to her. She had her cell phone on her lap, watching the show.

Someone cried out.

A lady with a slight hunch staggered through the crowd at the parking gate, pushing onlookers aside.

She ran over, her jade Buddha pendant swinging like a grandfather clock's pendulum. Quinn was sinking her teeth into an orange when she was ambushed by the embrace of her Bai Naoi.

"Where Marcie, she hurt?"

Marcie. She was still in the car. Seatbelt on. Clutching herself.

Linh marched up to the window. “Out, Marcie.” The girl sat there, biting her lip.She shook her head.

Linh tapped on the car window. “Out, *Nhu,*” She pried at the uncooperative door handle. She tapped the key remote. The door unlocked (thank goodness the unlocking mechanics were ok) and Linh opened it with such force that it seemed she would rip the door off.

“*Nhu*, you need to get out.” John had an old method of screaming for Marcie by her Vietnamese name (her legal middle name) to grab her attention. He was so commanding that even when he was hunched over his walker, he could ask Marcie to walk up to him so he could smack her.

“Your grandmother wants you out.”

She seemed as motionless as the corpses on the prairie during the Vietnam War. Linh’s heart nearly stopped. Marcie, could she have been unconscious? Did she suffer a head trauma?

Marcie’s eyes darted upwards, a sign the she was lucid, alive, unwounded. The flare in her eyes had been extinguished by the welling up of moisture. “Shut up, *mai.*”

She never said those words with placid serenity.

Linh’s hand rose, her eyes locked on Marcie in what she imagined how an enemy sniper would aim at his target. But then she thought of a blotched mark on Marcie’s cheek, two years back, when John physically chastised Marcie for stuffing flunked essays in the bottom of the recycling bin. Linh had feared then that Marcie would bear the dent of her father’s hands for eternity.

She opted to strike the ceiling of the car instead, causing a feeble *thwack*, sending a ripping sensation through her knuckles bones and the pearly sphere of her wedding band cracked.

Marcie gazed at her mother like an alarmed field mouse. Her hands fumbled with her seatbelt and her feet touched the pavement like those of a sore dancer regaining balance.

As Quinn wiped off her Bai Naoi, Ann's wet kisses, her grandmother patted Marcie's cheeks softly with both hands to rouse her from her semi-conscious state. The teenager began to shake her head as if to deflect an insect.

Linh rubbed her knuckles, letting the coolness of her left hand ease the pain, and yanked up a sleeve so the fabric could cushion it. "Get the girls into temple. I don't want them to miss the Dragons. I'll handle it from here." Maybe the Dragon can shower good luck on the girls. Linh brought her girls too much bad luck.

Ann grudgingly nodded, biting her wrinkled lips in a manner that could produce a sore. She had to be where John inherited his reprimanding attitude, the one he used whenever Marcie skipped school. Ann would take out her maternal austerity on Linh now that brain cancer had claimed her son.

Ann whisked her granddaughters into the parking gate and they disappeared among the crowd. Something jingled in the distance. The overture. The crowd turned into the gate, hurrying toward the sounds, realizing their truancy for the ritual. The thrashing drums chimed in. Linh remembered the sound of landmines exploding in the distance.

Midnight.

The Dragon Dance had begun.

The officer had been occupied with the Hispanic couple. The woman had dropped her vengeful expression and now wore a cordial, housewife smile, her arm draped around her husband's shoulders. They stood, tranquil yet shivering.

Finally the officer approached Linh, out of earshot of the couple.

Fixing his glasses, he flipped open his notepad. "You know they had the right of way."

"Yes, I should've..."

"They won't press charges though." From the way his head shifted, she couldn't tell if he was rolling his eyes.

"Oh." But now she felt she owed them more. "So kind." Buddha had blessed her.

"They won't." He yanked down his hat. "They can't. They're those Mexican illegals I bet. Praise Jesus. Or in your case, praise Buddha." There was a smirk beneath his glasses as he ripped out the sheet of paper.

She froze. She looked at the couple, biting their lips and talking in blurs of Spanish. Illegals? The ones on the news channels? The ones who climbed Texas borders to slave for dimes in sweaty yard jobs instead of salary-paying office jobs like John had? Paperless and ID-less illegals who might get shipped back over the Texas border back to their poverty?

Now Linh thought of riding the dreaded boats to the refugee camps, and how they could be turned away or whipped by the Communists patrolling the seas.

Dangling the citation over Linh's astonished face, the police continued, "Can't say for sure, but the guy's got no driver's license. Wife doesn't either. No papers on them. License plate's ain't registered." It was like the officer was adding those tidbits to reassure her. She could see her own perplexity in the reflection of the officer's glasses.

She phoned Triple A, pocketed the citations, snapped photos of the shambles of the motor and bumper in case insurance overlooked the full effects of the damage. There came the tow truck, to rig up her Honda.

There was no looking back as the officer tended to the Hispanic couple. She reminded herself to call up a taxi when all was done. She thought of their other car, the beat up, second-hand station wagon at home. Now there would be arrangements for her to drive both her girls to school. Marcie would never forgive her...

, toward the beShe strolled into the courtyardShe strolled into the courtyard, toward the beating drums, almost stopping by the fountain to gaze at the golden carp nibbling on the flakes of fish food. She flipped up her coat collar and looked to see if people stared at her. This was the right day to wear her mourning garb. No one looked at her. She was as invisible as the dark. The children cracked their firecrackers and the adults gossiped with monks. They weren't as scrutinizing as the kids in American grade school, who eyed foreign students that didn't know how to return the whispered offensive slurs.

She started ascending the stairs toward the entryway. She thought they might have closed the temple until she realized it was only the press of the crowd inside. She kicked off her leather loafers at the doorway. She spotted Ann's and Tom's slippers and the Nike sneakers of her daughters among the heap of the scandals, high heels, boots...

The Dragon emerged through the crowd. It exited the temple.

Yellow and crimson, it pranced on the porch, legs kicking up. The furry slippers of the puppeteers frolicked beneath the dragon's cocoon skin. Slithering like a snake, it weaved down the stairs past the giggling children and applauding families.

Then the Dragon stared at her, paralyzing her with its hypnotic, elaborate eyes. It flapped its jaw and she caught a glimpse of the puppeteer's eyes in the gaping mouth. It wobbled its great head like a whinnying horse. She remembered a time when John used to hold Marcie on his shoulder so she could touch the fuzzy head, like they were petting a pony. Linh listened to the fading revelry as the Dragon made a sharp turn and vanished, some children dashing after it.

She didn't know how long she stood on the porch, watching the vacant corner where the Dragon had turned. It was now parading elsewhere, impressing another face, startling another unsuspecting bystander.

The temple smelled like Vietnam with the scent of stale rice, rotten and fresh apples, pears, oranges, and soot.

The rug felt warm and fuzzy on her bare feet. Old scars flecked her soles.

Meditating on a Cherrywood desk, a giant Buddha sat poised at the central altar, cross-legged, half-asleep. Its brass was painted gold and polished, so even the patches of rust sparkled. His shrine was an uneaten feast of spotted and new fruits, rice, yeast cakes in plastic, and blocks of soy fish. Adults and children pushed incense into the ashes brass cauldron in the reciprical beneath Buddha.

If only the monks would renovate this temple. Nothing new. The floorboards, though polished, had tiny pits and the carpet at the altar was stiff from being vacuumed so many times.

No sign of the girls, Bai Noai, or Ong Naoi at the altar. They must have said prayers and gone to the memorial room. Without her. You always prayed to Buddha first before praying for your deceased loved ones.

She considered praying to Buddha, but her feet got to the back room before she could decide, she hoped they hadn't prayed at John's memorial without her.

The memorial room was crowded with pictures of deceased loved ones. Porcelain cups sat under each frame and held incense. The smoke smelled more pungent than the smoke from her broken car. John was among the dead who stared out at the attendance of their surviving family.

She could see her girls at the chestnut altar. Still lacking a definable expression, Marcie pocketed a gold-embroidered red envelope of cash, perhaps a hundred dollars for each girl, judging from previous outings with Ann. If there were qualities to appreciate about Ann, she sent Marcie and Quinn cash that could build their college funds. Maybe that's why Linh had put up with Ann for so long.

She came in just in time to overhear Ann say, "Don't be as careless as your mai or those Latinos."

Thomas, Ann's husband, was shaking his head. "Pray for good health. Your mother. Your father's spirit."

Tom's face lit up when he spotted Linh. "Oh my dear Linh, thank goodness you're here. Thank goodness the girls are alive."

He was like John, but infirm and hunched, like an old hound. John would have looked like that if he had have lived a few decades longer. He dragged himself toward Linh. He always wore his old uniform, re-patched by Ann's unsteady hands judging by the squiggle of seams. He smelled of fresh laundry detergent.

As John's passing was recent, his black-white photo was positioned on the center altar along with the other recently deceased. It was a black- and-white photo of him in his prom tux, robust and lively before the cancer claimed so many pounds of weight.

Quinn kneeled down before her father's frame. Ann pushed Marcie down with a hand on her shoulder, forcing her granddaughter to sink to her knees.

"Bow deeper." Ann mumbled. John had often complained about how his mother would hold him down so he could deepen his bow and insist that he bow more than the standard three times.

Tom muttered, "Thank goodness you and Vu's darling girls are fine. Oh Linh." He clasped his hands around hers. "No injuries. You're all fine." Though the man had a tender grip, she tried not to recoil from the searing pain in her knuckles.

"He had been watching you, us, my dear Vu." Vu was the original Vietnamese birth-name of John. "Vu was there. Still with us. With you. He saved my grandbabies. Remind his spirit that you love him."

She remembered John whispering to her, "I hated that name." Perhaps it was the one-syllable terseness of the language that drove him mad once he became exposed to the complex, "yet smarter sounding" English language. Although they had his burial spot engraved with "VU NGUYGEN," he never told his parents that he legally changed his name to "John Nguygen" and reduced "Vu" to a legal middle name that he never spoke about.

"Vu is here. Tell him you're safe."

Tom was so frail that she was afraid a heart attack or a stroke was always stirring in him. She could not break his heart. But she wanted to say that it was only the seatbelts and the sturdiness of the Latinos' truck that spared their lives and court bills.

She supposed John had saved them. Three years ago he had pushed for buying that Honda because of its high quality. But how could John have foreseen this crash? Surely it was pure coincidence that John had picked the right car. Pure coincidence they crashed into citizens incapable of taking court action against them.

Ann handed her a lit incense, the flaming tip drawing toward the bottom. Linh fidgeted with it. She disliked the smoke, stronger and more intimate than motor smoke, as smelly as John's ashes, but this ritual was the procedure.

Through the current of smoke, she could transfer her prayers to her husband into the afterlife.

Bowing in rhythm with her girls, she whispered, "*Nam no ai yi da fu,*" loud enough for Ann to hear and approve."*Gao min,* John, I mean, Vu." Ann had chided her for calling her son by his American name.

Really in her head, she was thinking of the Latino couple. She was praying to forgive the woman. She was praying that the cop wouldn't handcuff them. That they wouldn't be shipped back over the border. That the cop was wrong and that angry Latino-lady and her husband had only left their papers and licenses at home. That maybe if the cop searched their home he would find their papers in the drawers. She prayed the man's driver's license was on the kitchen table, right where he left it.

She stared back at John's beaming face, but she did not believe in his smile. She remembered a time when she wandered into a frame shop because American stores were like museums, displaying unaffordable items she could not touch. The Americans had a way of displaying sample pictures of models, a beaming blonde man with his brunette bride, deeply in love with no sight of divorce in their marital life. They made the pictures more appealing on the store shelves, but it was only after her high school years that she realized the couples in the frames were actors with a day job. She wondered why stores didn't advertise their empty frames instead of deceiving their customers that could be as well-off as the imaginary couples in the nine-dollars frames.

She chanted the well-wishes for John in afterlife, audibly so that Ann wouldn't scold her. She pictured it as a place so criminally white that she could not recognize the wisp of his ghost. What was he thinking there? Was he listless? Did he think of his girls? Was he so stubborn that he would try to rise from his own ashes and get through the granite funerary plaque with "Vu Nguyen?" Did he possess Marcie sometimes? Did he try to slap Marcie's face, driving her to unexplained tears?

When Linh and Quinn rose, Marcie was still on her ground, her face pressed to the carpet, her incense in her hands above her skull.

A muffled sob. Marcie gagged on her tears like she had at her father's funeral. She seemed unable to rise. Linh remembered Marcie's tear-stricken face as they pried her from her father's open casket before the undertakers nailed the lid shut. The riddle for the ages: was Marcie sad for her daddy, who once took her out to Putt-Putt for pizza and cheered louder than the other dads at soccer matches in her grade school years? Or did Marcie not know what to do with the freedom she had now, as if she had needed his screams and his merciless palms across her cheekbones.

Ignoring the concerned inquiries of John's devastated parents, Linh was distracted by Quinn, who was hovering her lit license in front of her, whisking the smoke toward Linh's nostril. Linh relieved Quinn of it. Then her younger daughter knelt down to Marcie and embraced her from behind.

Linh wanted to join in, but her hands were full. Even when she freed her hand by stabbing the incense into the flaky cake of ashes, she could not kneel to the stiff carpet to embrace Marcie beneath the visage of John. Rubbing her cold fingers on her blue-bruised knuckles, Linh only stood and watched alongside John's bewildered parents, as they all inhaled the smoke that clogged the prayers in their throats.

ABOUT THE AUTHOR

Caroline Cao is a Houstonian Earthling surviving under the fickle weather of Texas. When not angsting over her first poetry manuscript or screenplay pilot about space samurais, she enjoys acting in cheesy improve performances at BETA Theater, experimenting with ramen noodles and hollering vocal flash fics on Instagram. She runs a writing and scripting service and lends her voice to Birth Movies Death, Gurl, The Mary Sue and The Script Lab. She is MFA-bound for The New School in NYC.

Fair Return

By Kate Mock

FAIR RETURN

"THIS IS THE PEARL Arts District Station. Doors will open on the left. This is the Green Line."

Except the sign outside read "Buchanan" and the doors opened on the right. But this was indeed the Dart Rail Green Line. One out of three wasn't good, but it wasn't terrible either.

Brandon heard muttered cursing behind him, another glitch that needed to be fixed with the trains. Again he was glad he had insisted on limited runs before reopening the Dart line to the public. The last thing he needed was for people to get off at the wrong station and get lost.

Or not be able to get off at all, remembering what happened over the weekend. Three trains had just stopped in between different stations, their doors refusing to open. Just as well, since all of them had stopped on elevated tracks. The techs solved the issue after a couple of hours and no one was seriously affected by it. Although the raging winter winds left the travelers understandably scared for their safety.

An hour later and Brandon was at his desk, going over reports. He had been selected to rebuild the Metroplex area after the Collapse and subsequent Slaughter devastated not only the country but the entire world. But his focus was here; he took some comfort knowing others were doing their part rebuilding in other locations.

In little ol' Dallas, things weren't looking too bad overall. Downtown was still a mess but that had been true even before everything happened. No new injuries or fatalities from dismantling the unstable buildings. The museums were on track to reopen at the beginning of next month, and there was an approved application for a food truck, the first in years. He smiled. There were problems, but nothing that patience and creativity couldn't fix.

There were two other desks in the room with him, although only one was occupied at the moment. David was still north-ways trying to reestablish communications with communities near the border of Oklahoma. His other assistant, Markus, was frantically busy shuffling papers.

"Markus."

"Sir?"

"What have I said about delegation?"

The elf laid down the paperwork and sighed. "I need to trust the people under my supervision and let them do their job. Micromanagement creates more problems than solutions. I know, sir, I know. That's not my problem."

"Oh?"

Markus massaged his temples. "I'm trying to solve a resource and logistics problem and I'm no closer to a solution."

"What's the problem?"

"The Reclamation Department needs materials we don't have and there's a surplus of materials they need to get rid of. And I'm having no luck in finding a solution for either."

"What are our options?"

"Not many. The surplus is too valuable to just throw away. But...we don't really have any place to keep them short or long term. As for what the Department needs, it's in quantities greater than what they can salvage from any of the abandoned towns within a ten mile radius. I...I don't know where we can go to get them."

"Can they expand the radius? Like say, to a fifty or a hundred miles?"

"Not without threatening the new communities growing in the area. Also it's pretty untamed out there; David's people are still working to make transportation safer."

Brandon sighed in sympathy. They were trying to rebuild but so was everyone else, here and in the other worlds connected to the human one. Everyone needed supplies; getting them was the problem. Especially since no one wanted another war. Man and elf brainstormed different possibilities for the rest of the morning but were still no closer to a viable solution.

Brandon called a halt and went outside. He did some of his best thinking while moving around but Ami complained that his pacing set her nerves on edge. The landscape dropped him into a depressing, contemplative mood, erasing the hopeful tenor from earlier. Five years hadn't done much to erode the buildings here. H e could still recognize them for what they were, they had been built to last. But the only one seeing any use at the moment was the one his office was in.

The sadness and futility he normally kept at bay roared up. Did he really think he could ever make this work? Rebuilding the world to include magic and all that came with it when humans were so used to technology? Everyone and everything either destroyed or scattered. At times like this he cursed his commanding officer for saving his life and making sure he got back here. Maybe it would have been better for him to die on the field than waste away like this from despair and hopelessness.

Stepping into the shade of a doorway, Brandon leaned against the lintel and took deep breaths, fighting back the urge to sob.

"Brandon?" Markus stood nearby, a hand reaching out with concern.

"Sorry, sorry. Just...a little overwhelmed for a moment."

"No, no. It's okay. I'm sorry I mentioned my problems."

The human chuckled. "This has nothing to do with you."

"Then what..."

"This place, it has so many memories for me."

"Really?"

"Yeah, I grew up in Dallas, you know."

"You did?"

"Yeah, I guess that's one of the reasons why I was left in charge."

"I guess that makes sense." The elf cleared his throat, "So what's so special about this place?"

"Do you know why the train stop here is called Fair Park?"

"I thought it had something to do with your justice system or something."

This time Brandon laughed out loud, startling his companion. "No, no. That's not it at all. This, this is where the State Fair was held every year."

"State Fair?"

Brandon nodded, "Every state had their own version of it. It's a time to show off your green thumb, your animals, or crafting skills." He pointed to the building across the way. "Over there was the petting zoo."

"Petting zoo?"

"Saw animals there I didn't get to see anywhere else. Pay a small fee and you could feed most of them, too. Kids loved it." Brandon looked around with a glazed look in his eyes. "There was so much more here; rides, games, vendors, shows, demos, exhibitions, and so much food.

Markus let out a nervous laugh. "Sounds like an awful lot to cram into one day?"

"One day? Markus, the Texas State Fair ran for weeks, almost a month. Schools had Fair days for the younger grades and you could get discount tickets on certain days if you brought a specified item. And it was every day, not just weekends."

"It...it frankly sounds a little unbelievable, Brandon."

"It may to you, but it had a magic of its own no one could deny."

Markus looked around at the large, abandoned buildings and wide avenues. Guilt twisted the knife in his gut a few more degrees. The elves were outraged by humanity's actions towards the Fair Folk, yet his own kind hadn't been much different in their retaliation. They thought their righteous anger excused them for what they did. The screams still haunted his dreams at night.

Yet for all of humanity's cruelty, there was beauty, kindness, and wonder in ways his kind never thought of. He shook his head and sighed. So much had been lost on all sides. "I wish there was some way we could bring it back, Brandon."

"That would be nice. Let's head back to the office, Markus. We need to get back to work.

***

"Hey, is everything okay with him?" Ami managed to corner Markus as they waited for the train at the end of the day. The werefox secretary kept a maternal eye on both of them, which was annoying sometimes.

"Can't you tell? I thought your people could distinguish someone's health a mile away."

She flicked one of his long ears in annoyance. "One, that's wolves, not foxes. Secondly, that only applies to their romantic partners. Thirdly, you bloody well know all this already so stop dodging the question."

"He's...he's homesick." The elf explained the significance of the relocated government seat of the regent-elect. He clenched his hands to hide the oncoming shaking.

"Now stop right there, you're about to give yourself another guilt trip."

"Why not? This Fair was important to so many people. Why shouldn't I feel guilty for my part in destroying it?"

"Because unlike some of your kind, instead of holing up in your forest either lamenting or refusing to admit your guilt, you're actually trying to make amends for what happened. So. Seems like bringing back the Fair shouldn't be too hard."

"How? From what Brandon said, it sounds like a lot of work went into making it happen every year."

"I've got an idea. Let me make a few inquiries tonight and I'll talk with Brandon in the morning."

"Well, you sound confident enough. Good luck to you. But why are you taking such an interest?"

She smiled, "Oh come on. Who doesn't love a good party?"

***

"Ami, good to see you this morning. Markus mentioned you had a proposal for me. Let's have it." Brandon looked curiously at her.

"Thank you, sir. I understand this city hosted an event called the State Fair on these very grounds."

"That's correct, the Fair would last about three weeks."

"Well, I thought it would improve morale for everyone if it was brought back."

"No argument here. How do you propose to do it?"

"I'm afraid that's where I'm experiencing difficulty. I can't get anyone other than some humans interested. I guess it isn't interesting enough for non-humans to invest in. I'm sorry."

"Thanks, Ami. I'm glad you tried."

Sharp raps on the door interrupted anything else he might have said.

"Who is it?" Markus asked Ami as she checked the door.

She turned back to them with a wrinkled nose. "Goblins."

"Let them in, Ami."

"Wha— you can't be serious, Brandon. These are goblins."

"Ami, let them in."

She sighed in defeat at his tone and bowed her head, "Very well."

The door opened and a trio of short, green-skinned individuals came in and stood respectfully in front of his desk. Their clothes reminded Brandon of the steampunk cosplayers that posted their pictures on the Internet to show off their skill. He was also well aware that not all the other races thought well of goblins, though they mostly kept to themselves. Honestly he hadn't seen much of them himself since he approved giving them one of the warehouse buildings southwest of the city.

"How may I assist you today?"

"Well, sir, we heard some odd talk last night and wanted to know what you know about it."

"I'll try. What did you hear?"

Apparently Ami hadn't been too discreet when she was asking for support for the State Fair. The werefox blushed at the realization and hung her head in shame.

"I take it you have a problem with this?"

"You bet we do. It's infringement!"

"Excuse me?"

"We have no problem with a farmer's market; they focus on produce and other foodstuffs. But this Fair infringes on our ability to establish a Market."

"A Market?" He could hear the capital 'm' and was curious. "What kind of Market do you have in mind?"

The goblins explained. While it was called different things by different cultures, the Goblin Market was a place where anything could be bought or sold for a price, tangible or not. Fighting was allowed under strict, limited circumstances, otherwise violence was prohibited. Warmongering interfered with making a profit. The core of the Market was intensely magical, teleporting from one anchored location to another. It had survived the Collapse since its magic was independent of the ley lines. The goblin immigrants in Dallas hoped to establish an anchor for the Market in the city.

Brandon shot a quick look at Ami who nodded silently. What the goblins were telling him was accurate. He was quiet and leaned back in his chair with a loud creak. "How long would the Market be here in Dallas?"

One goblin shrugged, "Hard to say, a few days, maybe a week. Occasionally even longer than that."

"How reliable would the timing be? I mean if it's set to come for some days at a certain time of the year, would it hold to that and continue to show up at the same time for the same length?"

"Of course, sir," one of the goblins replied. "Doing otherwise would be bad business practice, hard to build up and keep a good customer base."

Brandon smiled and leaned forward with a thud that startled the others in the room. "Gentlemen, I believe I have a solution."

***

"Enjoying the view?" Ami asked Brandon.

He smiled and patted the step next to him.

She sat with a loud exhalation. "To be honest with you, I didn't think this was going to work."

"Really? Why's that?"

She shrugged, "Goblins just have such a bad reputation with the rest of us, it's hard to trust them and anything associated with them. They're so focused on making a profit."

"Doesn't sound too dissimilar with how some humans were in the old days. With what we're doing, everything is a risk. Giving the goblins a fair chance was just another one."

"Combining your State Fair with their Goblin Market," she said in wonder. "It seems to have paid off."

"Yeah."

All around them people walked along the thoroughfares, occasionally breaking off to join the crowds around different vendors or promotional booths. Some of the more traditional Fair features were replaced with unique vendors, courtesy of the Goblin Market. Brandon knew the Reclamations Department was happy with the arrangement; the Market allowed them to do a direct exchange for materials they needed with the surplus they had on hand. Not that getting this all together had been easy. Well, not too easy.

Once the goblins understood his idea they fell over themselves to help make it happen. They repaired and cleaned the buildings, handled the vendor applications and security. They also raised awareness of the Fair, catching the interest of more people than Ami had.

But a lot of the humans who wanted to participate in the various competitions couldn't for a variety of reasons; entries were few and often poor in quality. But Brandon was confident that next year would be better as they continued to rebuild and people could better prepare to compete. This was a good start.

"Hey, where's Markus? I thought the two of you were going to view your handiwork together."

"He's making himself sick," he replied.

"What?"

"One thing that always caught people's interest and attention in the old days was seeing what new food would be fried at the Fair. It was a competition between food vendors. Every year there was something new. Even impossible sounding concoctions like fried butter and fried beer."

"You're kidding."

"No, ma'am, I'm dead serious. Look at your map, it shows which vendors have them." He paused and his smile grew as her eyes did. "The sheer number and variety is incredible," he said.

"But why would they do something like that?"

He shrugged, "Because we could?"

Ami shook her head and laughed, "You humans, the most foolish and luckiest race in the entire multiverse. Not even leprechauns can match you."

Brandon chuckled. "Anyway, after Markus tasted the fried s'mores, he's gone to try every fried food here."

Ami winced. "And you?"

"I've already had my fill; I know my limit." He sighed and leaned back onto his elbows.

The fried s'mores hadn't been perfect, but it had been a good start.

Half an hour later a member of security found him; Markus had locked himself in a bathroom stall, sick to his stomach. Brandon shook his head and followed the goblin. There would always be some kind of hiccup as new things were tried out. But this was definitely a good start.

About the Author

Kate Mock, while born a West Point army brat in New York State, quickly adapted to Texas living and can't think of any other (real world) place she would rather be. She currently lives in Dallas with her husband and two cats.

Piano Lessons

By Rodney Walther

PIANO LESSONS

IRMA SCHUBERT'S GNARLED FINGERS unfolded the key cover of the old piano in her living room and trembled above the black and white keys. She could no longer bend her fingers like she wanted, due to her painful arthritis, but she was determined to play this morning even if it meant enduring swollen knuckles and stabbing pain in her wrist.

She ignored her aching hands and slowly plinked out the melody of *Amazing Grace*, the hymn that one of her students had played last year at her husband's funeral. On that day, the familiar music had poured mournfully from the pipes of the organ, swept through the sanctuary, and echoed off the smooth wooden pews and rough brick walls.

In the months since Preston's death, Irma had attended worship every Sunday in that same Methodist church near the banks of the Brazos River. She didn't necessarily find solace there—there was little comfort being so close to Preston and Rebecca, who both now rested in the adjoining cemetery—but she had promised the congregation she'd continue to serve as their organist.

Today, however, would mark the end of that commitment.

When she finished playing, tears welled in her eyes. All she wanted was to be with her family again. With shaky hands, she covered her face and hoped that when the time came, she could pry open the bottle of sleeping pills in her pocket.

Irma rose unsteadily, closing the piano's key cover out of long habit. She lumbered into the kitchen, retrieved a dish towel, and wiped her nose. She laid the towel on the table, bare except for an envelope she'd opened this morning. The envelope contained a letter from Walmart's real estate division. It concerned the twenty acres on which she lived. The land that had grown hay and nourished cattle for a half-century. The land that the retail giant valued at seven figures. The land that had killed Preston.

Irma knew plenty of widows. Her church overflowed with lonely women in their sixties and seventies. Her best friend Elizabeth, a soprano in the senior choir, lost her husband to a stroke the Christmas before last. Irma's own sister had spent twenty years living alone in the Texas Panhandle after Henry's death and was now battling pancreatic cancer. Irma had joined the widow's club six months ago when Preston unexpectedly died out in their field.

With her seventieth birthday long since passed, Irma couldn't understand why God still kept her around. Fifty-two years married to Preston, and he was gone. So too was their precious Rebecca, taken at age three by leukemia. Now Irma's own body was failing, clouded eyes and crippled fingers slowly stripping away her ability to play music.

Irma reached for the envelope, knowing she'd need to include it in her effects. She pulled the bottle from the pocket of her calico dress. Twenty pills. That should be enough.

Just then the doorbell chimed. "Go away," she muttered. "Let a woman die in peace." But the doorbell rang again, followed by three loud raps on the storm door. Her shoulders drooped and she gave a long sigh. She stuffed the pill bottle back in her pocket and shuffled to the front door, setting the envelope on the piano bench as she passed.

Opening the door, she saw a man in his mid-twenties with dark, close-cropped hair standing hand-in-hand with a pretty blonde about his age. They wore matching Aggie t-shirts pulled over faded denims. "Hello, ma'am. Mike Patterson. My wife Nancy."

"Can I help you?"

"We read about your farm. We're interested in making an offer."

"Sorry. It's off the market." At her instruction, the lawyer who handled Preston's probate had updated her will. With no living relatives save her dying sister, Irma planned to give everything to the church when she passed. And that time had arrived...as soon as she was able to send away these strangers.

Nancy slumped against her husband. Mike supported her arm and whispered, "It's okay. We'll find something else."

"Not that. Lightheaded...need to...sit down."

Before Irma knew it, Nancy's eyes rolled up in her head and her knees buckled. Mike caught her before she collapsed onto the front porch. "Talk to me, honey," he said, stroking her face. "Are you okay?"

Instantly, Irma's mind filled with images of Preston, limp and bloody, his eyes closing for the final time as she held him. "What's wrong?" she asked.

The woman groaned, and the man furrowed his brow. "It's never been this bad."

"Take her inside. Make her comfortable." Irma hurried to the kitchen, found a glass jar, and filled it with well water and four ice cubes. She returned to the living room, where Nancy lay sprawled on the couch. Irma handed her the jar of water and patted her hand.

"I'm so embarrassed," Nancy said.

"Don't be."

"Doctor said I needed to pace myself. Might be a rough nine months."

"Rest," Irma told her, remembering how nauseated she'd been in early pregnancy with Rebecca. "Take as much time as you need." She squeezed the pill bottle in her pocket. Soon she'd be with Rebecca again.

After a few minutes, Nancy regained her energy. Mike kissed her on the forehead and glanced out the window. "Real shame your place already sold."

"Didn't say it sold. Just decided not to sell the farm."

He frowned. "You know anything else around here for sale? Nancy and I are looking for a little farm to raise a family. Your place seems perfect."

Irma scoffed. This farm was the only home she'd known as an adult, and it was far from perfect. Her father-in-law had given her and Preston the twenty acres more than fifty years ago as a wedding present. They'd worked the land, cleared trees, installed barbed-wire fences, planted fields, raised livestock. They'd given everything they had. And what had the land returned? Droughts after the spring plantings, floods during the harvest, calf-killing coyotes, oak wilt. Then the final cruelty: that scorching September afternoon when Preston's tractor overturned, pinning him underneath.

She didn't blame God. Her faith was unwavering. She knew that everything they had was on loan, to be returned at His bidding. Preston. Her perfect Rebecca. The land itself. She understood that the church wouldn't use the property but rather sell it and put the proceeds in the general fund, and she almost wanted to live long enough to see the faces of the old men of the stewardship committee when they discovered Walmart's million-dollar offer.

"Me and my wife just graduated from A&M," Mike said. "Plan to do some farming and run some cattle. Maybe open a feed store."

"We both love the area here in Navasota. It's close to Aggieland. Plus, it has the rolling hills and bluebonnets."

"Yeah," Irma said absently.

"It's close to what you need, but far enough for privacy. Y'know?"

"Uh-huh." The man and his wife seemed nice, but Irma needed them to leave. She was late for her medication.

Nancy shifted to a sitting position and rested her head on Mike's shoulder. "I'm feeling better. We should probably go. Oh my God, is that a Bechstein piano? My mom used to have one of those!" Nancy rushed to the old upright and ran her hands along its intricate wooden details.

"Seen a lot of fingers stumble across its keys," Irma said. "Good for piano lessons, though. You play?"

"Yes, ma'am. I've played piano for years. Minored in music at college. Once the baby comes, I'd love to find part-time work at a church somewhere."

Irma felt an odd sense of déjà vu. After Rebecca's birth, Irma had become the organist at Immanuel Methodist, a job she'd held for forty years. That small paycheck, plus the money she received from teaching piano, had helped her and Preston make ends meet.

"Stay for a few minutes," Irma said, the invitation offered reflexively. "If you're up to it, would you play something? It'd be a treat for an old piano teacher." There was no need to rush things. After these two left, she would have plenty of time to carry out her final task.

"This is such a beautiful instrument." Nancy moved to the bench and accidentally knocked the envelope onto the floor.

"Just put that on top of the piano, dear."

Irma wondered if God had decided to summon this woman to her house for one final performance on the piano. If so, God must have loved music as much as she did. "Play something beautiful," she said.

Nancy played a simple scale, and her fingers danced across the ivory keys like Irma's had before the arthritis came on. Then the piano, which had known countless hands that butchered both hymn and sonata, softly sang out the tender *Clair de Lune*.

When she finished, Irma clapped with excitement, as she'd done with students through the years. "Oh, thank you! You have been blessed with a wonderful gift."

"You're very kind."

Irma could hear the notes resonating in her head, and she suddenly felt a lightness in her spirit that she'd forgotten existed. Months of confusing anger and guilt had long ago settled into a general malaise. The weariness she felt in her fingers and her bones seemed to have wrapped around her soul as well. Yet somehow music seemed to unlock that dark door.

"I guess we should leave," Nancy said. "Thank you for the water."

Mike stood. "We appreciate your hospitality. But she's right. We need to find us a place before growing season. And I still want to run by the tractor dealer today."

Irma thought of Preston and how much she hated his God-awful tractor. "Be careful," she said. "Those things are dangerous."

"Absolutely. I lost an uncle a few years back. He got caught up in a PTO shaft." Mike pantomimed a rotating motion with his hand.

"Dear Lord, that's awful."

"Can we please not talk about your uncle?" Nancy said. "It's too depressing."

Mike shrugged his shoulders. "Right. Sorry."

"Nancy," Irma said, trying to move past the awkwardness that hung in the air, "will you play something else?"

"Sure. How about this?" Nancy ran her fingers across the piano keys again with a speed and dexterity that Irma could only dream about. Then she launched into a cheery jazz tune. Irma recognized it immediately: Gershwin's *I Got Rhythm*.

As Nancy played, Irma could feel the upbeat music flow through her. A smile formed on her lips. "May I join you?" she asked, sitting beside Nancy on the piano bench. She relaxed her fingers and curled them gracefully above the keys. Nancy smiled at her and nodded. Then without missing a beat, Irma began to play.

It was as if she and Nancy had practiced the duet for years, as they played the song in perfect harmony, even executing the rhythm changes like seasoned pros. When it was over, they ended with a simultaneous flourish.

Laughter spilled from Irma, and she realized she hadn't allowed herself to feel this way in a long time. "That was fun!" she exclaimed.

"You're really good, ma'am."

"Call me Irma, dear." She thought about Preston and Rebecca again, and how music had intertwined their lives and drawn them closer. She remembered how they always used to sing as a family before bedtime, how she guided her daughter's tiny fingers to bang out the notes of *Jesus Loves Me This I Know*, how she hummed lullabies to soothe Rebecca after the chemo.

Irma had thought that God couldn't use a broken-down piano teacher. But she'd been wrong. Now she knew His plan. "If you're interested," she said. "I'd be open to selling the place."

Mike looked at her quizzically. "You said it wasn't for sale."

"Changed my mind. I like you two. Reminds me of when I was young and in love."

"What's the asking price? We don't have much money."

Irma thought for a moment, then said, "Let's see. Fifty years ago, this land went for a hundred dollars an acre. Going rate seems to be forty-five hundred to five thousand an acre. What would you say to ninety-five thousand for the house and twenty acres?" She knew that the county appraisal had been well over a hundred grand a couple of years ago, and that hadn't included the perceived value from Walmart.

"Ninety-five thousand? Seriously?" Mike looked at Nancy. Their faces spread into wide smiles.

"I'm too old to argue. If you think it's a fair price, I'll contact my attorney."

Nancy whispered to her husband and then looked at Irma. "When can we—?"

"Right away. You interested?"

They clasped hands and nodded.

Irma felt a sense of peace wash over her. "One more thing," she said. "Actually, two more things. First, Mike, don't you ever drive a tractor without wearing a seatbelt. And always keep it on flat ground."

"Sure thing," he said quickly.

"I'm quite serious," Irma said. "Promise me."

Mike met her gaze. "Yes, ma'am. I promise."

Irma plinked out a few more bars of *I Got Rhythm,* joy filling her heart and causing her foot to tap along. "And Nancy, I want you to have this piano."

"Really?"

"Play music, let your baby bang on the keys. Don't let it sit silent. By the way, I know a local Methodist church that needs an organist. Theirs is moving up to the Panhandle to take care of a sick relative."

Then Irma's arthritic hands pounded out the notes she played every week after the offering, the traditional congregational response to praise God for His many blessings. Soaking it all in, she placed the letter from Walmart on the keys and shut the cover. She closed her eyes and whispered, "Amen."

About the Author

A native Texan, **Rodney Walther** is the award-winning author of two bestselling novels (*Broken Laces* and *Space in the Heart*), emotional stories that weave together themes of regret, grief, and parenthood.

In his debut novel, *Broken Laces*, he merged the passions of managing baseball and of writing into a new endeavor, telling the touching story of a man who loses it all and then must discover how to become a better father...and a better man.

In *Space in the Heart*, he tells the story of an overprotective father who blames himself for a family tragedy, a vibrant newscaster who wants more than makeup and mirrors, and a wheelchair-bound teenage daughter who yearns for independence—all three characters connected by a shared history.

And he recently completed his third book! What *Remains Behind* is a romantic suspense novel that tells the story of a struggling single mom who accidentally kills an elderly couple after inadvertently taking a powerful medication. Then she falls in love with their surviving son. The problem? She knows the truth—he doesn't.

Known for his smooth narrative style and strong voice, Rodney has been recognized across the country with numerous awards for his fiction. He has been honored with first place awards from Houston Writers Guild, West Virginia Writers, Crested Butte Writers, Maryland Writers' Association, and others, plus has twice earned finalist status from the prestigious Writers' League of Texas.

Glowing reviews from readers and accolades from writing professionals show that Rodney Walther is a master craftsman and rising talent, a storyteller in the vein of Jodi Picoult, Jennifer Weiner, and Pat Conroy.

Broken Laces reached the Top 100 bestseller list for all Kindle books and stayed in the Amazon Top-1500 for more than nine months! *Space in the Heart* reached the Top 100 of all Kindle fiction in 2013.

When not writing, Rodney spends his time working as a business analyst, driving a tractor around his Texas ranch, or playing peekaboo with his grandson.

Padre

By Patricia Flaherty Pagan

PADRE

I SAT ON THE WARM SAND watching the apathetic waves wash away my plans and worries when the shot rang out. I had stolen a few moments of quiet from Mama's well-meaning monologues about the peace and celebration of nature to be found in the underappreciated hobby of birding. She got up deathly early every day, armed with enthusiasm and binoculars, and marched off to the nature preserve. You had to give her that.

My dog-eared copy of *An Unsuitable Job for a Woman* and open coffee mug full of margarita aside, the surf felt like my best therapy. Maybe it was okay that my mother had dragged me to an ornithologypalooza if this patch of near-empty beach and sea wind came with it.

"Enough with the résumés, this birding conference on the island is exactly what you need to get you out of your slump. They saw a Slate-throated Redstart on the preserve this week. Can you believe it?" Mama had asked me.

"Sounds nice, Mama, but I need to focus on getting a new job."

"By lying around in your messy condo in your pajamas drinking and watching *Dexter*? Which is much too violent for you to be watching anyway, young lady."

"How long is your conference?" I asked.

"A full week! That Dr. Jones from U of H is the keynote, too, and so handsome. You'll love it!" Mama exclaimed.

"He creeps me out."

"Well, experts from UT will be there too, Miss Picky."

Mama had hummed as she went online and reserved us two spots.

***

Bang!

Three young adults shattered my solitude as they tore by me on the windy beach. Two tanned, muscular, young white men ran by without turning. Then a young woman jogged by dragging one leg as if injured. She looked over her shoulder and caught my glance.

Do I know her? From where? She looks like crap. But kind of familiar.

Repulsive, a large, black bruise commandeered half of her face. I could see its full ugliness, even from five feet away. The hairs on the back of my neck prickled.

"Damn. Are you a Ruby kid?" I stood and called out to her before I could stop myself. A red blush of shame came over me at saying the words aloud. I accidently kicked over my morning margarita and tequila pooled in the sand.

"What? We're free now!" She yelled to the rough sea and me.

A Latina with a red scar on her cheek and long, shiny hair clad in a baggy beach cover-up jogged past me at the waterline. She approached the young woman with the bruise and gently tugged her away from me. They spoke.

Plop! The sound drew my attention to something small and black landing in the water. *A bag? A gun?*

"I threw that!" both women yelled. Then they laughed, tinny, nervous laughs, and waved. The woman with the scar ran away, baggy beach dress blowing in the wind, and the girl who might be a Ruby Kid, or a Ruby Kid look-a-like, lurched after her.

I froze for a minute under my beige Shoreline Inn beach umbrella. Rooted in the spot where sand reclaimed road, my body couldn't move until my mind untangled.

Could that really be the Ruby Kids after all this time? Crazy! But there were only three kids, not four. And what did the girl with the bruise mean by 'free now?'"

Dizzy, I squinted into the sun. Then I collapsed into a sitting position.

I don't believe in karma, do I?

Police car sirens blared toward me, and I wished for a strong coffee or another margarita.

***

Even the trio of brown pelicans perched on the edge of the bridge knew it was May, but the South Padre Island police station still smelled like spring break. The whiff of vomit, disinfectant cleaner with bleach, and suntan lotion refused to fade.

Sergeant Garcia handed me a Sprite. Beads of moisture trickled down the can. I fought the urge to press it against my sweaty forehead.

"Just to be clear, you are stating that you know the three youths and the Latina woman with the scar. And that you saw them all fleeing the scene in the same direction?"

I shrugged. "The young adults looked kind of familiar."

"And they all ran past you heading north?

Possibly running from the same location?" "I guess."

"You guess? A man is dead, Miss Kendall." Garcia drummed his fingers on the scratched imitation wood table.

"Maybe the right thing happens to the right person sometimes."

"I notice you're not so shaken up that Dr. Jones has departed this life."

I shifted in my seat.

"Let's focus on the three youths who were reportedly sighted on the beach that day. How do you know them?"

"I don't know them. I know *of* them. Everyone who worked in my old office does. We called them the Ruby Kids."

"The what?"

Folding my arms, I shook my head. "I shouldn't have said that. Listen, it's the confidentiality thing. You have to call my former supervisor."

"Your former supervisor at Harris County Child Protective Services." Garcia scanned a note he'd made, "Are either the victim or the woman from the beach linked to an open investigation?"

The nasty smell clinging to the walls was really starting to get to me. "You know I'm not supposed to tell you that."

The officer leaned forward. "I can get a court order."

"Please get one, but let me out of here, okay? This was supposed to be my vacation."

The sergeant's mouth pulled into a tight line. On the wall next to the camera the minute hand of the clock moved on.

"I can't help you. We've been going around in circles for over an hour. Do I need a lawyer?"

"You need to tell me exactly what you know about the history of the three young adults in question."

"Let's just say a certain former CPS worker, who shall remain nameless, back when she was on the intake desk, took a call from a local ER about a rich widower and U of H professor with a history of child abuse complaints against him. That night he'd brought in his tween daughter, who could barely walk, and two teenage sons. The kids were all painted red. Shining like rubies—I mean *covered* from head to toe in red house paint. Told the charge nurse that his Frappuccino-drinking, prep school-attending kids had been painting their own fence and fallen down the ladder. All three kids fell off the ladder into red paint. On the same day. While the nanny happened to be in the bathroom. The nanny hadn't said a word. Nurse saw a nasty scar on the nanny's face, too."

"Shit," Garcia said.

"Let's just say that this CPS worker, even though she was only on intake that day, would remember that case. Three kids beaten and then painted completely ruby red. She would remember the file that she pulled up on the computer, and the faces of the kids in the photos that were attached."

"I see. So maybe his kids got older, and stronger, and what goes around finally came around for Mr. Jones? Go on. Tell me more about what this widower did to this tween girl."

"Let's just say that the CPS worker never forgot the old photo of a tween girl with two broken arms a year before she mysteriously fell off a ladder, injured her leg, and ended up painted red. So, from time to time, this CPS worker asked after these kids, you know, generally, when talking with the appointed caseworker, who could have been named Jake Pham. She later left CPS, but remembered the Ruby Kids."

"I'll buy that." The investigator took his hands off the table and wiped them on his thighs, as if wiping off slime. "Why give them a name?"

"The caseworker said it once, and it stuck. You need a certain kind of dark sense of humor to make it at CPS. To keep your soul intact."

"And you say you saw the girl with the limp throw something into the water?"

"Yeah."

"What did she throw?"

"Something black."

Garcia leaned in. "Black like a gun?"

"Or a bag," I replied.

Garcia nodded and made a note. "You're free to go, but don't leave the island without letting me know."

***

When I finally got back to our blessedly well air-conditioned "suite" and saw that my mother was—*Praise the Lord*—off at a lecture, I threw some water into a pot and prepared to whip up some fresh shrimp, garlic, and pasta. The ocean-side birding conference Zen I'd hoped for had shattered the moment Garcia had mouthed the word "witness" to the female patrol officer on the beach. Feathered friends did not relax me. I needed a vacation from my vacation! My first instinct was to head home early, leave Mama to the Great Blue Heron, and spend the last three days of my break lying on the couch in my sweats watching vintage John Cusack movies and avoiding all human contact. Damn it. Garcia's warning and my cheapness dictated that I stay in the one-bedroom efficiency we'd booked with our hard earned cash.

After putting on some Jimmy Buffet, I stood before our open college-sized refrigerator lamenting my lack of Parmesan cheese. The suite phone bloop-blooped that we'd received a voicemail.

I dialed down the heat on the water and consulted the landline phone. During my seemingly endless visit to the police station, three different callers had left me the same message.

"I shot my father. He deserved it. For what he did to us. Tell the cops that you saw me."

So said each of the three distinct callers. Two male and one female. The hotel's caller ID confirmed that they had called from three different numbers.

All three of the Ruby Kids? How did they get our room number?

Rubbing my eyes with my hands, I shook my head. I turned off the burner and put my dinner ingredients away. I sighed.

Damn! I quit to get away from violence and to cut back on the rum. Now I stumble into this. Double damn.

Fifteen minutes later, I sat in the Bayside Bar where they were also playing Jimmy Buffet. Nibbling on Tilapia tacos, I gulped from a double Loco Pirata. As I waited on hold to tell Sergeant Garcia about the new evidence, I waved over the waitress to order another cocktail.

***

The courtroom smelled like Febreze and sweat.

"Tell us again, Miss Kendall, exactly what Miss Jones did when you saw her on the beach the morning of June the first."

I don't know what I expected, but Cameron County Assistant DA Didi Neyman looked plumper and more exhausted than the pit-bull prosecutors my fellow CPS workers had described. The bags under Neyman's eyes were carry-on size.

I yawned at the thought, and found myself wishing for more of the special breakfast Mama had made me that morning in the re-rented suite—her famous chicken and waffles.

"Funny. All of those cases you had back home, and you never ended up in court. Until after you quit, and went on a beach vacation." She handed the plate to me.

"Thanks, Mama. And yes, the irony has not escaped me. At least it will be over soon."

"Miss Kendall? What did you see the accused do?" Assistant DA Neyman's harsh tone jolted me out of my head and back into the courtroom. She paced back and forth in front of the witness box.

"She was trying to run, but her leg looked hurt. So she limped along."

"And she had a very large, black bruise on her face that you could see from where you were standing. Is that correct?"

"Yes, Ma'am." I strained to see if my former CPS supervisor had been able to come to court to back me up, like he'd said he would. But I only saw Garcia, sitting stiffly in the back of the courtroom. And then, towards the front, I thought I glimpsed the woman with the scar on her face. I squinted.

It's her! The nanny.

The former nanny and close friend of the Jones children, whom the newspapers would identify as Ms. Esperanza Ruiz, wept into a wad of pink tissues. Wearing a billowy flowered maternity dress, she hardly resembled the fourth runner I'd seen on the beach, except for the scar. She sobbed so loudly that the people seated around her turned to look at her as well.

She never left me a voicemail.

"And Miss Jones spoke to you?" Neyman walked up to the witness box and stood as close to me as she could. Her large nose loomed disturbingly close to mine.

"No. I called out to her. I thought I recognized her, and I was surprised. I didn't mean to, but I asked her if she was one of the kids who'd been painted red. I blurted it out."

"Please confirm that you refer to the way in which the Jones children were painted red by their father, Mr. Jones, as was previously stated by Jake Pham, their former case worker. And that you learned about the Jones family through your former employment with Harris County Child Protective Services."

"Yes, Ma'am. That's what I meant."

"Did Miss Jones answer you?" My hands itched to push the lawyer's big old nose out of my face.

"Did she answer you?"

"Not really. She said 'What?' like she didn't understand."

"And then?"

"Then she said 'We're free now."

"And what do you think Miss Jones meant by that?"

"I don't know." I frowned.

"After that statement, what did you see her do?"

"She threw something in the water, and then she dragged off after the others."

Neyman flashed a triumphant smile. "This object that she threw...would you say that it was the approximate size of a gun?"

An older woman sitting in the courtroom gasped. I saw Garcia lean forward.

"Well..." I stalled, butterflies swarming in my stomach. *How could I be sure? How much had I had to drink that morning on the beach?* "I guess it could have been."

The nanny wailed. Out of the corner of my eye, I could see three jurors writing things down.

Miss Jones sat up straight in her seat, giving the jurors a poker face.

"If it was a gun, I could see why."

"Excuse me, Miss?" the Assistant DA asked with a dismissive wave of her hand, walking back towards her seat.

"We are, all of us, better off without him," I said.

"Objection. The witness is testifying. Thank you miss, you may step down."

***

A month later, I lay on a deck chair under the afternoon sun with an open copy of Christie's *A Caribbean Mystery*. As I stretched out my freshly-pedicured feet, I spotted a pregnant woman. She shone in the full bloom of pregnancy. She shuffled by me in a white and gold beaded maternity shift looking like a sun-kissed Madonna. You could tell that she was wearing foundation, but there was a hint of a red mark on her cheek. To tell the truth, I was sipping my third frozen mimosa of the day, and it would take a damn-good make-up job to cover that scar, but I was seventy-five percent sure it was Esperanza Ruiz I saw walking on the Fiesta Deck.

What the hell?

My worried mama had splurged on the cruise out of Galveston as a little respite after the Jones trial. Even Mama, who was sure everything happened for a reason, could not see why God's plan did not include her exhausted, unmarried daughter taking a few days of rest now and then. Rest that might give her the energy to start dating again. Rest that might offer better stress relief than the clan of empty Becker wine bottles taking over the recycle bin. Rest that did not include witnessing the murder of a child abuser. So, out came Mama's Visa, and we packed our bags.

Mama clapped her hands while she talked about snorkeling in blue waters, and I grinned like a fool whenever I saw the stack of paperback Maron and Christie novels on the nightstand in our cabin.

"There's so much we can do!" Mama said.

"Or not do," I added.

Blessed nothing was what I was doing when I maybe saw Esperanza Ruiz that sunny afternoon. I'm sixty-five percent sure it was her. As she, her heavy make-up, and her giant belly floated angelically toward the elevator to the ship's spa, she spoke to someone. Probably me.

"My baby will be an angel, not a ruby," she said.

Sitting up abruptly, I started to ask, "What about the gun?" but she disappeared into a window-ringed elevator.

"What about what dear?" Mama asked from beside me, lowering her new, purple-rimmed sunglasses from Buc-ees.

"Nothing, Mama."

Turning my head, I couldn't see the nanny in the elevator anymore.

"Are you sure you're okay, Honey? Maybe you should switch to lemonade."

Am I okay?

Stirring the red straw in my yellow frozen drink, I mulled it over. Maybe the young Jones daughter whom I'd testified against and her two older brothers had acted like so many bold island waves, washing the truth away. Maybe a case with three confessions had been just as hard for Garcia to investigate as "a case" with none. Maybe the Jones girl had purposely thrown the gun. The gun that someone else staying in the beach house had shot.

Oh my God! What if it was never about the damn past? What if it was about the future?

A seagull cried in the sky above the ship. Mama applied sweet smelling coconut oil sunscreen to her arms. I sipped my yummy frozen orange juice and sparkling wine. The scent of grilled shrimp and fresh mangoes filled the air as dinner preparations began. Yes, this nagging doubt that the right woman had gone to jail should definitely have riled up my moral sensibilities. It quite possibly had me, in my tipsy state, seeing the possible killer in a perfectly innocent pregnant woman. Eggs Benedict from brunch still lay heavily in my tummy, but my mouth watered.

The Ruby Kids stayed silent. Why shouldn't I? Marking my page with a bookmark, I shut my mystery novel and stood.

"Mama, you up for table tennis?"

About the Author

Patricia Flaherty Pagan loves writing and reading about complex female-identifying characters. She is the author of *Trail Ways Pilgrims: Stories* and the writer of award winning literary and crime short stories such as *Bargaining* and *Blood-red Geraniums*. She edited three collections of fiction by or about women: *Approaching Footsteps, Eve's Requiem* and *Up, Do: Flash Fiction by Women Writers*. She teaches flash fiction writing at Writespace in Houston.

Learn more about her upcoming releases and events on her website: www.patriciaflahertypagan.com. Follow her on Twitter @PFwriteright.

Armadillo Paradise

By Winston Roberts

ARMADILLO PARADISE

HE HAD MADE IT to the smooth ground: the black ground with the white stripes down the middle. It was said that this ground was holy. The Creator had built the smooth ground to test the armadillos - to see who was worthy. Only the Chosen could make it to the other side.

He heard them coming before he saw them. They were fast moving boxes sitting on black round things. They whooshed by at amazing speeds. If you were caught on the smooth ground when one of them came, you were toast. He squinted his eyes as it passed; they kicked up a lot of sand as they went by.

He basked in the Texas summer heat. The sun was high in the sky and would give no succor with its searing flames. He liked the heat, it was much preferable to winter's chill. Another box was approaching. He could tell from the vibrations through his feet. It was a big one this time; one of those with 18 round black things. The ground shuddered as it passed. He hunched down to avoid being driven back by the wash the box threw on its way.

"Murph!" Murph was short for Murphy. It was his friend, Al.

"Hey Al! How ya doin'?"

Al lumbered up beside him. "Same-o. What y'all doin' here?" Al looked up and down the expanse of smooth ground.

Murph decided he was checking to see if any boxes were approaching, too.

"Dunno. I might be thinkin' of making a run."

Al looked at Murph with a suspicious countenance. "You crazy?"

Murph had expected this response. How many of their friends and family had lost their lives trying to make the other side of the smooth ground? Murph turned to Al and smiled. "Maybe."

Murph went on to explain himself. "The old ones tell tales of the other side of the smooth ground. They say that there was a time when the smooth ground didn't exist. Armadillos could travel from here to there unimpeded. The land beyond the smooth ground has a river of water running through it with trees lining the sides. "

"That's just an ole campfire tale!" Al was not a believer.

"They say that when the fruit trees by the river drop their fruit they are covered in the fattest, juiciest maggots. The beetles are so round you can't eat them in one bite. They say that years ago one of the Armadillos over there made it here. He got curious as to what was over that there smooth ground and made it all the way here. And what's more..." Murph paused for effect, looking over his shoulder to make sure they weren't heard. "They have ladies!"

"Well if you ain't just the biggest armor plated idgit in the whole entire world!" Al laughed at his friend. "There ain't no sech thing!"

"There are to!" Murph was getting a bit peeved at his buddy.

"That's just a horse barn of hooey! Besides, we got us some fine ladies here!"

It was Murph's turn to laugh. "What, old lady Turnbull? She's so old she got dinosaur teeth marks on her shell!"

"What about Daisy? Daisy would be quite a catch."

"She's got a boyfriend, and he's a real donkey's ass!", said Murph.

Al had to admit that Daisy's boyfriend, Richie, was a bit of a halfwit. "Well there's always Amy."

Al was reaching now. "Amy's nice but what she got growing between her toes? Looks like leprosy or somethin'!" Murph was adamant. "Admit it, there just ain't no good prospects for us on this side of the smooth."

Al nodded his head in agreement. Murph lowered his voice and, in whispered tones, confessed. "I'm lonely Al. I want the wife and a den under the big live oak. I want to watch the kids playing in the grass, chasing the grasshoppers."

Al bumped his friend with his shell. "Well you always got me, buddy."

Murph sighed the sigh of a being resigned to an unwanted fate. "Yeah, but I'm not sure I'm ready to go full on homodillo."

Al chuckled. "Yep, you right. I don't think you got the fashion sense for that." They both laughed.

They sat in silence watching the boxes roar by them, some going this way, some that.

Finally Al broke their reverie. "Hey, ain't that Ernie over there?" Murph nodded agreement. "Hey, Ernie!"

"I don't think he heard you...ERNIE!" Ernie either didn't hear them or he was ignoring them. The boys sat with rapt attention as they watched Ernie flip his head this way and then the other, waiting for his opportunity to make his run.

"I think he's going to run!" Murph turned to Al, excited and concerned at the same time. Ernie flexed his muscles in his legs and in one great leap jumped onto the smooth ground.

Simultaneous to Ernie's leap, Murph felt the telltale vibrations in his feet. A box was coming!

"Ernie, BOX!" The boys shouted with all of their lungs. They needn't have wasted their breath, though. Ernie already knew he was in trouble. Ernie froze and then in a tragic failure of decision making, turned to return to their side of the smooth ground.

"Roll, Erine, ROLL!" Al knew he could roll faster than run.

Ernie grabbed his hind feet with his front feet and started his roll to the side when, in a mighty whoosh, the box ran over him. It had been one of the 18 round black things boxes.

Murph and Al ran to their friend's aid. What awaited them was the silhouette of what had been Ernie, but in a much wider, flatter form. The boys sat by the smooth ground for quite a while, silent in reverent reflection of the loss they had just taken.

"Well at least he tried." Murph was trying to find the positive.

"We never know when it be our turn." Al wiped some moisture from his eyes.

The boys turned to leave. Al swished his tail at Murph. "Hey! You wanna go down by the cactus garden? I found a coupla crickets there t'other day."

"Sure, I guess." Murph was shaken. Suppose that had been him instead of Ernie. "No fire ants, though. I've still got indigestion from them we had yesterday."

The duo waddled off into a gorgeous sunset. The quest for Armadillo paradise would have to wait for another day.

About the Author

Winston Roberts is an AI/Robotics experiment gone very wrong. He is currently living underground in escape of his human overlords. Or, maybe, Winston Roberts is a very lucky man who married his trophy wife as his first wife. They live in Indianapolis with their cat who doesn't care. He has two amazing kids in whom he is fiercely proud.

The Devil Prays the Rosary

By James Lesadeau

THE DEVIL PRAYS THE ROSARY

ALCOHOL IS THE LUBRICANT of the past, always has been, always will be. Without lubrication, memories grind up against each other, hard, cold, metal-to-metal, and seize—like a piston in a cylinder never to move again. With proper lubrication, memories go up and down and round and round forever, like painted ponies on the carousel.

I came here every anniversary since I was old enough to drink, to relive the day and the night in my mind's eye. The Great Storm of 1900 changed Galveston forever, from a place of commerce to a place of recreation. And it changed me.

I sat in the bar of the Hotel Galvez, the casement windows allowing the gulf breeze to ease in unfettered. It was a fine, upscale bar, with beautiful green and white tile checker-boarded across the floor, and rich mahogany trimming the creamy plaster walls. In the corners and against the walls, large false castors and dracaena and ficus trees cooled the room pleasantly and contrasted handsomely with the main wall, which was made from brightly colored bricks—red, peat brown, orange and dark purple. From the ceilings, large, ornate chandeliers bathed the room in a soft glow at night and a refined grace during the day. The smartly-clad waitresses were Splash Day contestants, who were assured a fine living for the rest of their lives from having participated in a beauty pageant, and not just any beauty pageant but the oldest one in America. Atlantic City would beg to differ, but let them beg and let them differ. These girls looked like a million tax free bucks.

The air was tinged with salt and gasoline and mystery. Across the palm tree-laden lawn, a streetcar clanked to a stop in front of the hotel on Seawall Boulevard—but no one got off. Across the bar a young couple, in their early twenties, was laughing and touching each other. Behind me there was a solitary middle-aged man reading *The Galveston Daily News*. He talked to himself conversationally, asking and answering questions with gestures of surprise and recognition. There was a young family, a husband with his wife and two daughters, both young and pixyish, with pony tails hanging from their heads and bangs hanging in their eyes. They played pattycake. When one or the other missed, they smiled together. A bellman wheeled a large cart with ten or twelve trunks on it. I could hardly imagine traveling with so much baggage. A man leaned in the doorway as he rolled past. He had a face like a half- eaten apple pie.

I finished my drink, a Manhattan, and signaled for another. I like mine with rye whiskey, but they made it with bourbon whiskey here. It was late in the evening of September 8, 1946. The war was over, and America was ready for good times. Galveston transformed from a military base to a tourist destination, and folks from all over the country poured in. The season had just ended, and yet there had been no drop-off in traffic. The Hotel Galvez was called the " Queen of the South," though she looked more like a European castle than an American hotel.

I was an orphan at St Mary's Orphans Asylum on Galveston Island. My parents died during the yellow fever epidemic. I had watched them go: yellow eyes and skin, black vomit, and finally brown piss as the liver and kidneys shut down. The Catholic Church stepped in to care for the orphaned children, or at least that was the story I was told. I was six when they died and by the time I got to St Mary's I was a spunky eleven-year-old boy, red haired and freckled, with skin white as alabaster.

The day began oddly from the start, as a dark and threatening sky. It had been beautiful just the day before. I was given detention that fateful day for fighting with one of the other kids who had stolen my dessert. Everyone played along, pretending nothing had happened, but I caught him later that night in the bathroom. I gave him a nice shiner. Revenge came at a price.

Father Daniel arrived the next morning by train. After hearing the story, he took me in the back for a belt whipping. In "the Room." Everyone dreaded "the Room." I pulled my pants down for the whipping, and took it standing up and without crying, but then Father Daniel covered my mouth with his hand, pushed me onto the floor, pulled my skivvies down, and raped me. It was the first, and as it turned out, only time.

***

As I drank in the present and my Manhattan, my mind wandered to memories of Mary Tyler, my first friend at St. Mary's. She was a pretty girl who liked to brush her long silky hair. She hinted that the nuns did sexual things to her and the rest of the girls. She hated them for it. She killed herself exactly one year before the day of the hurricane, on September 8, 1899. I remember the date because she was discovered one day later, the date on her tombstone would have been 9/9/99. The day before, she had cursed the orphanage in front of the entire mess hall. "I curse this place, I hope it washes into the sea, I hope God comes and takes all of you, and dashes your heads against the rocks. I curse this place. I curse it!"

They found her hanging from the rafters the next day in her white shirt and gray gabardine skirt. Before she jumped to her death, she tied ropes to a long board like two slings, and slid her arms into them, so that when she jumped she hung there like a crucifix - suspended, spinning slowly one way, then back the other; her haughty baleful eyes open wide and staring out over the mess hall. Her mouth was agape and flies buzzed around her in the still, stifling heat. The faint odor of death hung in the air like garlands on a Christmas tree.

***

"That'll teach you to behave, Eric," Father Daniel told me. The memory of Father Daniel's voice brought me back from the ghastly image. "You know you deserved that, for what you did. Do you realize where you would be without the church? You would be on the streets, begging for food, sleeping in alleys, with no one there to care for you when you get sick or need help. Is that what you want? You have to understand that what we do here is for your own good. We will have harmony and *order*!"

These men *of God* were taking something precious from us. They preyed on orphans. Mary Tyler said children who complained disappeared. Father Daniel was evil incarnate, outwardly pious but inwardly a ravenous wolf. She said the church used human sacrifice to achieve their ends. That was how it worked. "Who do you think they make those offerings to?" she asked, her eyes dull and distant. "God? Why do you think these people become priests and nuns?"

"Father Daniel...how could you do that to me?" I asked sniffling. I sat confused about what I should be feeling. Fear, anger and shame seemed natural, but I was too afraid to be angry and too angry to be ashamed.

Father Daniels began again. "Be thankful you have a place to call home. Whatever happens in here is nothing compared to out there. Now pull up your pants, clean yourself up, and not a word to anyone." He sneered at me and said, "Who'd ever believe a little runt like you anyway?"

With a broken heart, I reached down and pulled up my pants. The windowless room reeked of dirty laundry and fresh paint. I looked around blinking, and single tear rolled down my cheek and fell to the floor.

He opened the door and glanced both ways before yanking me out of "the Room." We walked down the dark, foreboding hall toward the light of the mess hall, past the kitchen and its swinging doors. The cooks and kitchen help stared at me with forlorn faces. I knew that they knew.

"Sister Theresa. How are you doing?" Father Daniel asked stepping into the light of the mess hall.

"I'm fine, Father Daniel," she said beaming. "I'm headed into town. Would you like to accompany me? I need to go to the infirmary." In her hands were Rosary beads. Whenever she sat alone, she plowed through beads and prayers with machine precision.

The night before Mary Tyler killed herself. I walked downstairs, and there alone in a corner of the mess hall, Mary Tyler was on her knees hissing at something between her legs. As I approached her from behind, I saw what she was cursing. There on the floor was Sister Theresa's Rosary beads soaked in blood.

"I would like to accompany you," Father Daniel replied. "I have some business there myself." He paused, looking down at me, saying, "I don't think you'll have any more trouble out of Eric. He's a good boy."

The air turned cool and feathery light and smelled like flowers.

"That's good, Eric," said Sister Theresa. "I want you to go to your room and think about what Father Daniel told you. And no sulking!" She pointed a crooked finger in the air, raising and twisting it threateningly. Her eyes radiated malevolence and her message was clear: she could make that happen again.

"Yes, ma'am." I walked out of the mess hall and toward the stairs. I climbed them and walked down the hall to my room. Time followed close behind, like a monstrous pet snail.

"What's with you?" my roommate, Larry, asked.

"Nothing."

"It happened to you didn't it?" he asked.

"Yeah, I guess it did." I walked over to the sink to wash my face. I felt dirty. I looked in the mirror. I didn't look the same. My freckled face was no longer that of a boy; my youth was gone—stolen— but I wasn't an adult, I was in between.

"It happens to everyone," Larry said. "Jeremy set you up."

We didn't say much the rest of the afternoon. I fell asleep crying. When I awoke late that evening, I heard a word I never heard before: hurricane. The word traveled through the dormitory like an electric current. Everyone was running up and down the halls, telling each other about it, whispering what it meant, and praying. The nuns were organized. They were busy boarding up all the windows from the inside. It was the best they could do. They ordered the kids to carry as much food as they could upstairs.

"Sister, why are we staying here? Why don't we go to the

hospital?" I asked.

"Hush, Eric," Sister Theresa said sternly. "We know what we're doing. The hospital is full to overflowing. There's no room there."

I walked to the back door. I wasn't sure I wanted to see what was outside. I could already hear it, smell it, and taste it. I opened the door and walked outside. The once-blue sky was as dark as the night, sanguine marked with ugly with streaks of red and green stringers hanging from the darkness to the sea below. The clouds rolled, roiled, and rumbled like a frightful cauldron of anger, rage, and hate; a monster from heaven come down to stir the sea. A stone's throw away, the waves were ten feet high and crashing ashore, and darkness was falling with the speed of a guillotine.

I ran back in screaming "Sister, we have to get out of here! We have to leave! We have to get out of here now!" My stomach melted like cotton candy.

Sister Theresa grabbed me like a rag doll and dragged me down the hall again.

"Let me go! Let me go! Let me go!"

When we reached the back closet next to " the Room," she turned and grabbed me by both shoulders and set me down upright.

"I'm not going to have a panic on my hands," said the Sister. "Do you understand, Eric? If you can't behave, if you can't lend a hand, then in the closet you go."

She shoved me down hard into the closet, and I landed on a pile of paint-stained, smelly, oily rags. By the time I recovered, I heard the lock click close and her footsteps fade away.

"Help! Help! Help!" I screamed. I had to get out of there, but how? I knew if I stayed there I was dead. I felt around the dirty rags, around the floor. Nothing. I ran my hand to each corner, and it was there that I found it—a crowbar. I picked it up and struck the doorknob hard, again and again. I heard someone cry out and knew time was short. I lay the crowbar against the knob with the long end sticking out, using the frame of the door as a fulcrum. Holding the jimmy with my left hand, I raised my right leg up and kicked it as hard as I could, then again, and again. "C'mon!" Finally it broke and the door opened.

My legs were noodles inside my dungarees, and I shivered

in my sleeveless t-shirt. Goose pimples rose on my shoulders and forearms. I stumbled forward to see what was happening outside. I opened the back door and the water was there. The beach was gone. The wind screamed like a wild animal, carrying choking screams and chilling cries for help.

I ran over to the stairs and heard the boys and girls with the nuns upstairs singing "Queen of the Waves."

***

"Sir, would you like something to eat?" a voice asked.

"Huh?" I asked, looking into the face of the barkeep.

"Well, it's getting late. Would you like some dinner? We have some fine red snapper, caught fresh today. The chef filled it with crab and oyster stuffing and a hollandaise sauce on top. I must say, sir, it is delicious."

The present swirled together as if pulled through a vortex in time. I came back in a huff, my mind trying to grasp the culinary intricacies being thrust at me by this insolent, ruddy faced barkeep with bad breath.

"Uh sure. Yeah, that'd be great. Maybe a little red wine," I said, turning my head so as not to smell his breath.

"May I be so bold as to recommend the white?" asked the bartender. "We have a nice Chardonnay that would go perfectly with the fish, sir."

"Great, give me one more Manhattan while I wait." I cleared my throat.

The bartender quickly fixed the libation, placed it before me, and then walked toward the kitchen. As he did, I saw him raise a hand to his mouth and smell.

***

Queen of the Waves, look forth across the ocean. From north to south, from east to stormy west, See how the waters with tumultuous motion Rise up and foam without a pause or rest.

There were six inches of water in the mess hall. I ran up a few steps, stopped by the light of two small kerosene lamps. I saw the nuns with the boys and girls in the hallway tying them together with rope.

"Get a loop around all of you," Sister Theresa commanded. "Everyone that wants to live has to be tied together with us. No, no, no not like that. Tie a good strong knot. If we get washed away, our only chance to survive is to stick together. We've got to make it to higher ground, while we still can."

The orphans pleaded, "What do you mean washed away? We're safe here right? RIGHT? Sister, I am so scared! Oh, Sister, please don't let us die, please don't let us die!"

The wind howled demonically. Many of the girls screamed in terror.

"Shut up," Sister Theresa hissed. "Do you hear me? Silence! We must keep our wits about us if we are to survive. No more screaming!"

The children sobbed even worse after that, their tiny chests heaving and gulping for air, then bawling and shaking uncontrollably.

I knew I didn't have a chance with them. It was every boy for himself.

But fear we not, tho' storm clouds round us gather,

Thou art our Mother and thy little Child Is the All Merciful, our loving Brother God of the sea and of the tempest wild.

I ran downstairs toward the door. The sea crashed it open with a wave and I was staring at open sea. I saw pieces of wood and bodies floating outside. A stray boat crashed into the side of the dorm. Everyone screamed. A brilliant burst of lightning flashed across the sky and illuminated the gruesome water filled with every imaginable human trapping: from clothes and firewood to chairs and tableware, from hats and shoes to sofas and beds, from bodies of people and swimming dogs, to pieces of buildings and houses. I heard a loud bang, then another. I held on to the doorframe and looked outside. The wind scoured my eyes nearly shut. The ocean lifted the dormitory next to us, up, and then slammed it down, up, and then down again. Every time it settled, it settled with a thud. The outer clapboard wrinkled like an old woman's face.

Help, then sweet Queen, in our exceeding danger, By thy seven griefs, in pity Lady save;

Think of the Babe that slept within the manger And help us now, dear Lady of the Wave.

Everyone was screaming now, although a word or line could

sometimes be heard. A large wave crashed against the dorm and swept me back all the way to the mess hall. I never saw it coming. I reached and pulled for the surface but got caught between a wagon and a large wooden chest.

The back wall was now gone, the emptiness framed the oncoming storm like a huge picture. I grabbed onto the chest and held on. It was full and it was heavy but it was floating.

Again I heard the thud of the next door dormitory being pounded to the ground. With every thud I heard screams. Finally the last thud, and the entire dormitory crashed into the sea, sounding like the end of the world. The water was now 5 feet high and I could no longer touch bottom. I kicked my legs frantically to get out of the main building where I was and where Sister Theresa had tied the children together at the top of the stairs.

Up to thy shrine we look and see the glimmer Thy votive lamp sheds down on us afar;

Light of our eyes, oh let it ne'er grow dimmer, Till in the sky we hail the morning star.

Behind me, Sister Theresa had come down the stairs to get a look. Her eyes held a look of terror. She had waited too long to make her move. The tying of the rope had taken too long. She saw me in the water.

"Eric, come here!" she shrieked.

I could see the rope leading up the stairs, attached to some other poor soul. I pretended not to hear her. She thought to lead the string of children through the water toward the front door. The water was too high. She realized they were trapped, and I saw death pass over her face, like a cloud over the moon.

"Eric! ERIC! Come here!"

I clutched the chest and kicked and pushed my way out of the building we were in, and found myself in the ocean. The water was almost halfway up the side of the building. I knew they would never make it out. Horrified, I watched the orphanage do exactly what the dormitory did, pounding up and down and finally collapsing into the sea. There were a few lights in the distance. I bumped into a huge oak tree trunk. I let the chest that saved me slip away and climbed on top of the tree. A new surge of water carried me across the vanquished island and into the bay. Nothing that I knew remained, just open water.

***

"Here you go sir," said the pig-nosed bartender, tiny veins splayed map-like across his snout. He looked at me and perhaps though he had awakened me from a dream.

"Ahh, looks delicious," I replied, picking up a napkin.

"Hope you enjoy it sir," he said.

I picked at the crab and tasted it. I was hungry. That much whiskey can get the hunger gnawing at your stomach like a beaver on a tender hackberry.

"And here is the white wine as promised, sir."

"Thank you, barkeep. What is your name, so I won't have to continue using that dismal title?"

"My name? Why, Matthew, sir."

"Thank you, Matthew. Oh...my compliments to the chef."

"Thank you sir. I will offer them immediately."

***

Then joyful hearts shall kneel around thine altar And grateful psalms re-echo down the nave; Never our faith in thy sweet power can falter, Mother of God, our Lady of the Wave.

Finally the eye of the storm settled over me and I heard tiny little voices in the calm air. "Help! Help!"

"Who's there?" I yelled.

"Larry and John. We made it out. Is that you, Eric?"

"Swim over," I replied. "I'm on a tree trunk. I can save you. C'mon, swim!"

"I can't make it," one of them replied. "My legs are too tired." "You can make it," I said determinedly. "Swim with everything you've got."

They struggled mightily through the waves for nearly half an hour. Finally, I could reach them one by one and pull them onto the tree trunk. They had been clinging to an empty coffin. We hugged and kissed each other in the eerie calm, the jagged darkness of the sea all around us. We used our belts to strap each other to the tree as best we could. Soon, the back half of the storm came down upon us. We were being swept out to sea now, back across the island again. The storm hammered us, and we screamed and cursed and sang and cried.

The tempest began to subside. Off to the east, we saw a glimmer of light—the first light of dawn. It would reveal an ocean strewn with bodies and debris as far as the eyes could see. It looked like all of Galveston was in the water. I recognized the roof of the train station bobbing, and the steeple of the church, and even the sign from one of the big saloons. The rain ebbed and we drifted toward the shore, slowly at first, and then at a steady pace. The town's remains were headed back with us. I thought I could almost walk across it, like a rat skimming a fence line.

Galveston was gone except for a smattering of buildings clustered around downtown. We stood on the tree trunk surveying the grisly scene. The feeling of being alive when everyone else was dead was like winning a poker hand when everyone else folded. You wanted to think you won something, but the truth was everyone else had just given up.

We climbed off the tree and waded over and through the wreckage. Dead people were scattered randomly through the debris field, tucked here and there like Easter eggs hidden in the woods. We walked through the debris for at least an hour before we saw another living soul, a deaf handyman from the town named George.

It was then we walked up on the first of the nuns and orphans from the orphanage. They were strewn in and around an old house that had grabbed the line they were all tied to and taken them down, drowning all of them like a forgotten stringer of fish. The children's faces were contorted into clown-like masks, frozen in the horror and disbelief.

We walked for hours and saw nothing but dead bodies and mountains of debris, two, sometimes three stories high, eerily bobbing like a gigantic cork. It was around then we heard the moans and screams of people trapped in the rubble, unable to move or dig their way out. We scrambled to move parts of the wreckage to uncover those trapped. Some were lucky. Others we could not get to. Tired, weak and drained of any hope, the realization some would never escape overcame us. We had no choice to but to rest, then keep moving.

Finally, we came upon Sister Theresa. She had two

children in her arms clutched tightly to her bosom. The rest of the kids, eleven in all, tied neatly behind her. Together, they looked like a string of Rosary beads only the devil could make.

***

"How's that fish sir?" a voice interrupted. It was Matthew's, of course. "I hope it is to your liking?"

I stuttered for a second, my mouth half open with food. "Yes, it is quite good," I said. "Maybe a little more cayenne pepper. Otherwise, it is excellent."

"I'm glad you like it sir," Matthew said.

***

It was late in the day. We walked, climbed and swam for hours, with no food or water, the screams of the imprisoned and dying searing our ears. We were getting desperate. We knew we had to make it to town. There was no saving anyone else—we had to save ourselves. Soon we began to hear the noise of the town and we all breathed a sigh of relief.

We stepped onto the first solid ground when we reached the outskirts of town. There were water and food stations set up, and long lines waited at each. They took pity on us as we walked into town, revenants that we were, and we were brought to the head of the line.

Everyone looked horrendous. The term that would come to define this state of mind had not been coined yet, but would have to wait for a world war: *shell-shocked*. We had been hit with a force beyond our comprehension.

Someone came into the town and said the train had been thrown from its tracks with no known survivors. She pointed in the general direction where it could be found. I decided to see if I could determine Father Daniel's fate. I walked along the bay until I came to the train station. I passed it on my way to the end of the line. The bridge was ripped away and the train had fallen into the bay. There were a few bodies lying around. A gigantic locomotive had fallen off the bridge and was laying there, an anchor in the sand. The rest of the rail cars were gone. I walked down to the edge and looked over the side. There, impaled upon a piece of iron track, was Father Daniel.

***

"How's that red snapper sir? It looks tasty. You mind if I try some?" asked a young priest who had come and sat down next to me. He was reaching with his fork to take some food from my plate.

"Yeah, I do mind," I said crossing over his arm and driving it into the bar.

"No offense, fellow. I just noticed you were through eating, that's all," he said, grinning.

"I wasn't through eating. I was thinking," I said coldly, looking into impossibly familiar eyes.

He smiled and said, "You know this is the anniversary of the Great Storm, the one that killed 12,000 people, the worst natural disaster in the history of the country."

"Really? No I didn't know," I replied, taking a sip of wine. "You think something like that could ever happen again?"

"I don't think it ever stops," he said. "Death created time so it could grow the things it would kill."

"Hmmm. Did corruption create innocence so that it would have something to steal?"

"I've never heard that one, but I see what you mean. Death and corruption...two sides of the same coin; you cannot deal in one and not the other. It's the basis of the Catholic Church." He got up to leave. "Enjoy the rest of your meal. My apologies for the intrusion."

"I will, Father," I replied. "But tell me something. What brings you here? To Galveston?

He smiled, started to walk away, then turned and said, "Did you know that the word hurricane comes from the Caribbean God of evil? More precisely, Hurakan, the Mayan God of wind and storm."

"No I didn't," I said. He turned and walked away, disappearing into the night.

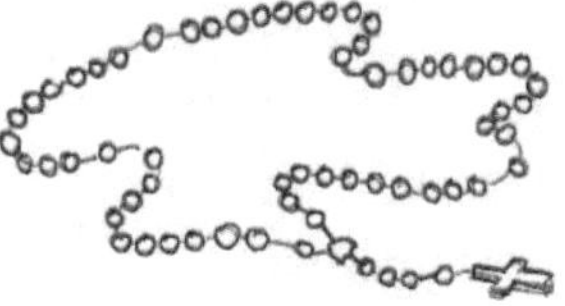

About the Author

James Lesadeau was born in New Orleans, LA. He grew up in Metairie, LA, a suburb of New Orleans. He went to Louisiana Tech University where he studied Mechanical Engineering. He has worked as an engineer in both the aerospace and oil & gas industries. He has written off and on for the last 20 years, but recently has gotten serious about it. He has studied the craft in great detail, and is currently writing a series of short stories will be anthologized in *The Conspiracy Railroad*. He is also writing a trilogy of novels called *Pirates of the Milky Way*, which will delve into the golden age of pirates and how they may have been instrumental in the founding of America. He currently lives in Houston, TX and works in the oil & gas industry.

The Legend of Woman Hollering Creek

By Sabrina Eads

THE LEGEND OF WOMAN HOLLERING CREEK

I ARRIVED AT THE HOSPICE facility about 20 minutes late for my volunteer shift. I hadn't wanted to volunteer here in the first place, but the food bank and school volunteer sites were already taken. I was trying to get extra credit for a course I was taking in my last year of graduate school, and the teacher was a real do-gooder type. I hadn't done as well as I would have liked on one of our research papers, and I wanted to get an A, so I decided to join the volunteer project.

Dr. Cheek explained that we would volunteer a minimum of 40 hours to bring one grade up to an A. It seemed like a lot of work, but I felt like I needed the boost and I figured it might be a good thing to fluff up a resume, considering my career choice.

I walked into the staff restroom, and grabbed a set of the scrubs we were required to wear at this facility. I changed out of my tomboyish jeans and tank top, it being 95 degrees in Texas in early December, and into the drab brown scrubs that had been laundered probably hundreds of times. They were comfortable, but not too comfortable. I secured my long hair into a tight bun, and made my way to the charge station.

"Good morning," I said to the nurse, Verna, who would give me my task for the two-and-a-half-hour block I signed up for.

"You're late," she said flatly. "Just 'cause you're a volunteer doesn't mean we don't notice."

"Sorry, Verna, I won't let it happen again," I said. I couldn't promise I wouldn't, though.

"Yeah, well. OK, Rose, Mrs. Velasquez in room ten needs company. No one has stopped in all week."

"What's her situation?" I asked as politely as I could. "Well, she's been on palliative care for about 2 weeks. She has stage four ovarian cancer. Her relatives live in Idaho, and she just has one friend in this city, who hasn't been able to make it in. She's very lonely, and stops us nurses to chat quite a bit. Which, we don't mind when we don't have rounds, or something we have to work on, but lately, we've had a lot of patients leave us, and a lot of grieving families, and...we're short staffed, so if you could just sit with her for a while and talk to her, or let her talk."

"Sure," I said, feeling nervous. What does one say to a stranger who's dying? But I forced my feet to march into room ten. I knocked before I entered. I said, "Hello, Mrs. Velasquez?"

She had been reading, and wore those glasses that are sold at drug stores for folks who need magnification for reading. These particular ones had tie-dye purple frames, which made me smile. Mrs. Velasquez was in her sixties, I'd estimate, and she had steel-gray hair, which was long. It went down her back and looked to have been recently brushed out. She was thin and bore the characteristic hollowness of someone ravaged by the effects of chemotherapy. Within moments I determined the hair was most likely a wig. Despite her obvious illness, she wore make-up and was dressed in jeans and a light pink blouse with fluttery sleeves. Her clothes hung off of her, though she'd clearly been a rather small woman even before the cancer. She was sitting in an overstuffed arm chair instead of in her hospital bed, though she had a cane nearby to help her maneuver.

Before I had a chance to enter the room, she queried "Yes?"

"My name is Rose. I'm a volunteer here. I thought I'd check on you, to see if you'd like some company. I see you're reading. Do you mind if I ask what you're reading?"

"Not at all, dear, come in."

I sat in a chair next to her. She showed me the cover. *Woman Hollering Creek, and Other Stories*, by Sandra Cisneros.

"I've read that," I said. "It was very good."

"I thought I'd try it out, see how close she got, considering I am descended from the woman the creek was named after."

Puzzled, I asked, "How can that be? I thought that it was about a pioneer woman who haunts the place after having drowned her kids to save them from an attack by natives. She then went mad."

Mrs. Velasquez laughed. "No, dear. Way back my family settled these parts. We're the descendants of the woman. Her name was, of course, Maria."

"So then, she must not have drowned her children, or at least not all of them," I said.

"That's right. Maria didn't lose her children, the children lost Maria."

Then Mrs. Velasquez told me the story. Maria and her husband had been settlers, not too far off from the creek. Maria had always been a little different than the other women, but her husband did not mind her peculiarities. No one remembered what those quirks were, exactly, but she had been different.

When Maria had her first baby, a girl they named Concepción, Maria cried for two solid weeks after the birth. A curandera, or healer, happened to travel through their area and they'd heard tell of it through their church. Maria's husband had asked for something to help Maria be able to return to her usual self, and be able to stop crying and enjoy her daughter.

The curandera, an old woman, who had been called a witch by many, came to Maria's home, and fed Maria her homebrewed soup. She put Maria to bed after giving her a calming draught, and cared for Concepción while Maria's husband tended to the property, the livestock, and the land.

Maria was also provided with a tea that she was to take for three days morning and evening. The curandera also gave Maria some help for her swollen breasts which wasn't the least of Maria's physical complaints, but the curandera knew that if Maria was able to feed and quiet her child, that would help her to remain calm.

After a week of careful tending, the curandera had to leave, but gave Maria and her husband instructions for everyone's well-being. The curandera was paid in goods, produce, and a quantity of dried meat for her journey.

Maria continued to have children. Each time she became a mother, the resultant tears and grief after the births grew more and more desperate. The curandera came back several times, through two boys, and a set of twin girls, but she was an old woman and eventually died. The curandera had taught Concepción how to care for women who were experiencing the same things her mother experienced as children came, but she was quite young and did not have much experience. Concepción did the best she could, but after three more children, Maria was found in the creek, drowned, several heavy rocks tied to her legs and arms.

Her children mourned with the simple, innocent grief of children losing a mother. The three youngest were unsure what had happened, and knew only that Concepción had taken the role of mother for them, and they cried because everyone else did. Maria's husband cried, and when he was through, he took his wife's bloated corpse and buried her 200 yards from the creek. He marked the grave with a stone he found that was foreign to the area, having been brought by someone, or some creature.

For three years, Maria's husband gathered wildflowers weekly and brought them to her grave. Then, one spring, he announced he planned to marry a woman from the church. She was his daughter Concepción's age.

Her name was Violante. Maria's husband had fallen in love with her youth and beauty. He needed someone to care for the children, as Concepción had reached the age when she was to marry, and begin having her own children.

Concepción was opposed to her father's marriage. However, she offered no objections aloud.

Early one morning at the witching hour when all were asleep, Concepción crept to her mother's grave. She wept and told her mother of the torment she felt having another woman take her mother's place. Concepción felt a chill. A sudden fog rose from her mother's grave. A terrible wail of grief, hatred, betrayal, and loneliness deafened Concepción. For a moment, she was so disoriented and terror-stricken, she thought she had been struck deaf permanently, until she heard the sound of weeping that did not come from her mouth.

A hazy image stood before Concepción. She felt instinctively calmer. She knew it was her mother's spirit. The image stated she would never harm those who loved her, but those who interfered in their family were to be made sorry for their actions. The haze moved away from her, toward the house, then vanished.

Over the next several nights, Maria's husband heard weeping, wailing, and other sounds of anguish. He was soon to be Violante's husband. Every evening, he awoke and saw a hazy figure and felt disquieted. He began to lose sleep.

Violante also was disturbed in her slumber. During the day, she dropped glass containers full of food, she ruined her mother's provisions, which angered her mother.

One day she was sent out to fetch water at the creek. She saw the mist rise up and take the shape of her fiancé's deceased wife. She fell into a dead faint. Her husband to be found her in this state.

Violante explained her recent shock, and her fiance shared his disquiet. They agreed that it was best if they do not tell anyone else, and decided they would still marry.

On the evening of the wedding, Violante fell ill with a fever. Her father thought it was because she had been lying on the cold ground for so many hours. He felt certain that she would recover. He sent his daughter to the home of her new family, where Concepción tended her. Days turned into weeks, and Violante remained ill. No one could quite say what was wrong with her, other than delirium, a fever, and no appetite.

Violante quietly faded away.

Maria's husband went to the grave of his first wife, and apologized. The betrayal, though, was too deep, and Maria's spirit continued to haunt the creek, disturbing her husband's slumber, causing him to look wild-eyed and sleepless. The priest dismissed his concerns, but as Maria's husband became more and more wild, the priest visited the home. He witnessed firsthand the mist and heard the spirit's anguish at having been supplanted. He never again visited the property, and somehow, the story began circulating around the area that the creek was a place filled with foreboding. Those who did visit the creek never were quite the same afterward.

Even now there is an air of despair and anguish surrounding the property.

"After the death of Concepción, her grandchildren, and great-great-grandchildren report the area remains one of mystery. The women in my family are all told, on their wedding day, the story and of how our vows may be 'til death do us part,' but our history shows the power of love from beyond this world, and that we must continue to honor the ones we love even after they are gone," said Mrs. Velasquez.

I sat on a folding chair, rapt at the story. Mrs. Velasquez blinked, and suddenly looked ten years older.

"Dear, I am feeling a bit tired all of the sudden," she said. "Could you help me get into bed?"

I assisted her into her bed, and tucked her in. She was still wearing her clothing, but said she didn't mind. She didn't have the energy anymore to sit up.

"Mrs. Velasquez, do you have any children?" I asked, as I made ready to leave.

"No dear, I never did have any children."

I smiled at her, and thanked her for the beautiful story.

"You're welcome, dear. I hope I see you again soon." She drifted off to sleep.

I left when my shift was over. I wasn't scheduled again until later the next week to finish out my hours.

"Hey, Verna," I said by way of greeting, as I walked up to the charge station ready for my shift. "Does Mrs. Velasquez need any company this week?"

"No, Rose. I'm sorry, but she died last Wednesday. She left something with your name on it, though."

Verna handed me a small note. It said, "My first name is Concepción, after the first Concepción in the story. I hope you will remember me, and remember the story, and pass it on." On the note was an illustration of what Concepción Velasquez believed Maria looked like in life, and in spirit.

I felt shaken and emotionally unable to handle any further events that day. I left without finishing my shift.

I slept, and dreamed of Mrs. Velasquez, asking me to remember her and tell her story.

When I awoke from my nap, I went to the scene of the story, Woman Hollering Creek, and gathered some twigs, rocks, and a tiny vial of water. I set up an altar of sorts using the twigs to craft two rings intertwined, and placed them, the rocks, and the vial of water along with the note and a plate holding a yellow candle, for remembering.

I sat at my small desk, and wrote this story. I hope you pass it on.

About the Author

Sabrina Eads lives in Houston, Texas, and has lived in the surrounding area for over 30 years, since the age of 3. Writing has been a lifelong passion, and after a hiatus of about 10 years during which she was establishing a career in a different line of work, she has returned to the avocation with aplomb. Sabrina has dabbled in the writing world, including running an online journal collective, searching.org, now defunct, with monthly topics, writing and running a 'zine distribution organization, a short stint copy editing at the University of Houston's newspaper, *The Daily Cougar*, and a volunteer gig at the University of Houston's literary magazine, *Gulf Coast*.

Texas Potty Training

By William M. Barnes

TEXAS POTTY TRAINING

IT WAS WASH DAY. That morning, Daddy drew buckets of water from the cistern. He heated it in a black pot over a fire and filled the washtub. Then he cranked the motor on the washing machine. It was loud, kinda like his car.

Mama poured soap powder into the hot water and put in some dirty clothes. "Turner, did you kill that wasp nest under the seat in the johnny like I asked you to? You know how those awful things scare me."

"Sorry honey, I forgot. I promise I'll do it tonight." He kissed her on the cheek and walked down the alley to open his drugstore for the day.

Mama worked all morning, washing the clothes and hanging them on the line. When she was finished, she took me out back to the johnny.

I was learning to pee-pee like the big boys do without wetting my socks. "If I learn to pooh-pooh potty, can I wear big boy panties"

"Sure can."

When I was through, it was Mama's turn so I played in the sand just outside the door. That's when I saw the snake.

I played with my cars and trucks in the shade of a mesquite tree while Mama used the outdoor johnny.

Grandpa always called it a 'two-holer'.

"Mama?"

"I'll be out in a minute, Billy Mac. Play with your toys."

"Are you doing pee-pee or pooh-pooh?"

"Never mind. You shouldn't ask questions like that."

"Mama?"

"What?"

"What does a rattlesnake look like?"

"I'll show you a picture of one when I get through. Now play quietly."

"Does he look kinda gray with pictures on his back?"

"I guess so."

"Mama?"

"What is it?"

"I think one just crawled in there with you."

I didn't hear a thing for what must have been a full minute.

Then Mama yelled, "Billy Mac, don't move!"

"Why?"

"Run to the house and bring me a hoe."

"You said don't move."

"I know, but I changed my mind."

"Why?"

"Never mind. Run to the house and bring me a hoe, quick."

"Why?"

"I'm gonna kill this snake, that's why. Now hurry up!"

I couldn't find a hoe so I brought her a hammer.

"I told you to bring me a hoe."

"I couldn't find it. Where's the snake, Mama?"

"His tail is under my foot and the rest of him is under the seat, somewhere."

"Why do you have your foot on his tail?"

"I don't know - I just do."

"I wanna see." I peeked inside.

She dropped the hammer and stopped me with one hand, holding a roll of toilet paper with the other. Her foot was on the snake's tail.

"Stay outside!"

"Why?"

"Do as I say!"

I went outside.

In a minute, she said, “Billy Mac, come back inside.”

“Why?”

“Don’t ask questions, just come inside.”

She still had one foot on the snake’s tail, her panties around the other foot and a hand full of rusty nails.

“Hand me that hammer.”

“Why?”

I’d seen that look on her face before. I handed her the hammer.

Mama nailed that snake's tail to the floor. I don’t know how many nails she used but it was a lot. Then she grabbed my arm and marched me to the house. "Stay on the porch and don’t move."

I didn’t ask why that time. I just watched.

She found the hoe and ran back to the johnny. When she stuck the hoe through the hole in the seat to kill the snake, a whole bunch of wasps flew out. “Oww! Oww!” she yelled.

She ran out of the johnny so fast she knocked the clothesline to the ground. The clothes were dragged a bit in the mud. She grabbed up the dirty clothes and took them in the house, all the time swatting at the wasps.

She tied a rag to a stick, soaked it in coal oil and ran back to the johnny. She lit the rag on fire and tried to burn the wasp nest. They stung her again and she dropped the rag.

Then the johnny caught fire. She drew water from the cistern and tried to put out the fire but she was too late.

She came back to the porch. “Billy Mac, do you see these two things?”

“Yes ma’am.”

She held them in front of me. “This is a hammer, this is a hoe. This is a hammer, this is a hoe.”

By this time, my socks were wet again.

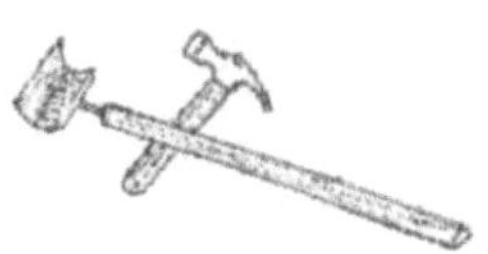

Mama made me sit on a stool in the bad boy corner next to the dirty laundry while she cooked supper.

When Daddy came home, I watched him walk real slow past where the johnny had been.

There was nothing left but a pile of smoking ashes, a hole in the ground and a terrified snake, hanging by his tail and looking down at a whole lot of...yucky stuff.

Daddy slowly stuck his head through the back door. Mama stirred a pot of boiling beans.

Her face was all swelled up and smeared with white lard.

He tiptoed over and kissed her on the cheek, then wiped the lard off his lips. "Guess I should have killed that wasp nest, huh?"

Nobody said much during supper.

We all used the slop jar to pee-pee in that night.

***

Early next morning, Daddy slipped out to the car and drove off. He came back later with some lumber.

Mama watched him unload. “Didn’t you open the store today?”

“No, Honey. I had some errands to run.”

He put up a new clothesline and helped Mama rewash the clothes. The next day, he built a new johnny and painted it red.

When the paint was dry, he called me. “Billy Mac, come out here for a minute.”

He opened the door and pulled me inside. “Son,” he said. “I’ve taught you the adult method of pee-peeing and you’re doing quite well in the pooh-pooh department. Now here’s something else for you to learn.

He lifted me on his lap. “Your mother is a woman. Some day you will marry one of ‘em.

Always do what that woman says and don’t ever ask why. And if she tells you to kill a wasp nest, for God’s sake do it.”

***

It turned out I married a woman. I killed every wasp nest she told me to kill and I never wet my socks. I know the difference between a hammer and a hoe and I never had to re-build a damned johnny.

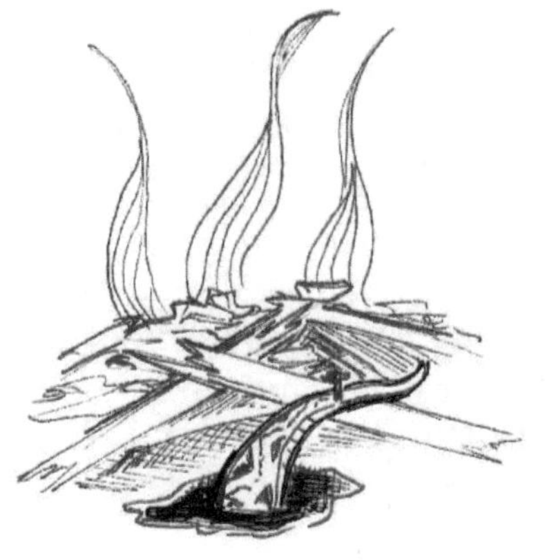

About the Author

William "Bill" McCargo Barnes, 87, was born on June 10, 1929 in Anson, Texas, a small sleepy town with a population of 2,000. His father worked at the local drugstore until the family relocated to Grandfalls, an even smaller town of just 500 where his father opened his own drugstore. He attended Sul Ross State University in Alpine, Texas where he earned his B.S. in Geology before serving in the U.S. Army. With over 60 years in oil exploration, he decided to start writing at the age of 65 and was met with success. Author of the *Nonesuch Chronicles,* a collection of short stories as well as additional works set in Southwestern locales like Mexico and Texas. He passed away peacefully with family by his side on April 12, 2017.

Bill was well known for his quick wit, sharp mind, deep compassion and devotion to his family and friends. He was an accomplished writer and loved sharing critiques with fellow authors. His letters-to-the-editor on political topics are legendary.

Pretty Green Eyes

By Chris Rogers

PRETTY GREEN EYES

WHEN THE SHOVEL BLADE refused to pierce the hard Texas ground with a first push, Betsy tried again. This time she placed her sneakered foot on the blade's upper rim and stood on it with all her weight, and this time the shovel bit deeper. She lifted out a small plug of turf and soil.

The deed was started. She swallowed a woolly lump in her throat and shoved the blade into the ground near the same spot as before.

"Are you sure you don't want help with that, Bets?" Dad asked.

He hovered nearby with his own shovel, but Butch was Betsy's dog and it was all her fault that... so it was her job to...

She swallowed again. *To bury him.* "Thanks, Dad. I can do it."

"I know you can, sweetheart, but I don't mind—"

"I *want* to do it. Butch was a good dog."

"All right, then. Yell if you need me."

"Okay."

Her make-believe smile felt real enough on her lips, and it brightened Dad's sad eyes a tad. The smile of a teen, she noted, setting her shovel again, *almost* a teenager, the smile of a girl twelve-and-a-half, old enough to shoulder the burd—

Her throat closed up. Tears threatened.

...the burden of responsibility. There, a safe enough word, a neutral word. *Responsibility.*

She stood on the shovel again and dug out another chunk of the hard ground. Dad was still watching, pretending to be busy, so she gave him a better smile this time, a thoroughly capable smile, maybe a little triumphant. It worked.

Dad smiled back. "You've got it, Queenie." He sort of waved his shovel as he walked toward the house.

Her dad always knew how to make things better. Dad told her when she was about five that, by naming her Elizabeth, he and her mother had gifted their first born with choosing whoever she wanted to be. From the name Elizabeth, you could abstract any number of other names, each with its own personality and character. Beth, Betty, Betsy, Liz, Liza, Leeza, Lizzy, and a host of others, including Queen or Queenie, because Elizabeth was a favorite name for queens. Later, Betsy looked it up. Five Queen Elizabeths in England alone, if you included both the regents and the consorts. When Betsy attempted a particularly difficult challenge, a "queenly" challenge, Dad called her Queenie.

She rammed the shovel into the ground again, realizing she now had a hole about the right length and width for Butch's little coffin, which Dad made. Now she only had to dig the hole deeper.

Before she turned twelve she could handle responsibilities. Walking to the bus stop alone came when she was six. Making her own lunch when she turned eight. Babysitting her little brother when she turned twelve. Now this: one more duty on the way to being a grownup.

The cool breath of October fluttered around her, lifting dead leaves that fell from the magnolia tree. Messy trees, magnolias. They didn't save up leaves until autumn. Instead they dropped them all year long. Cones, too, like pine trees, though she knew from science class they were properly called "fruit," because they contained seeds. They were Butch's favorite thing to play catch with.

When he was a pup, Butch could jump and catch a cone in the air. More recently, he would let it fall before grabbing it, but always with enthusiasm and a sense of pride, as if retrieving that cone was his duty, no matter how often Betsy threw it away.

PRETTY GREEN EYES

Butch was pretty old, more than eighty in dog years. Dad told her when they were both six months old, Betsy saw Butch at an adoption fair and wanted him. They became best friends. He wouldn't have lived much longer, maybe, but he didn't deserve to be smacked down by a drunk teenager driving fast and crazy on their sleepy neighborhood street. Betsy was quick to get the license plate number, though she knew the car on sight, having seen it ripping along the main drive many times when she took Butch for a walk. But they hadn't been walking that day. Butch was off his leash and spied a squirrel, and... *if Betsy had been watching him closer...*She wouldn't be digging this hole.

Thunk! Her shovel hit something metallic. When she lifted the dirt out, a wisp of dust twirled upward and a piece of shiny metal glittered.

Kneeling, Betsy picked it out of the soil. "Oh!"

Warm. It was a pretty silver crucifix, but why was it warm? The soil was cool. Too big to wear around her neck, but maybe she could ask Dad to attach it to Butch's marker.

His *grave* marker—she had to get used to that word. She was digging a *grave*, a hole where her best friend would lie for eternity. She set the cross aside.

"I'm not sure it's legal to bury an animal in the yard," Mom had said. "Maybe we should ask the home owners association."

"And you can be damn sure what their answer will be," Dad argued. "Never mind what's legal, it'll be forbidden in the HOA's ninety-seven page document. So don't ask. It's our yard. We have the right to decide what we do on our own property. Was it legal for that kid to be driving drunk? What if it was a child he ran down?"

Mom looked thoughtful. "He'll be punished, but that doesn't answer our dilemma."

"No dilemma! Betsy and Butch have been together since they were both babies, and I'm not taking him away to be thrown in a furnace."

They didn't know Betsy was listening. That was the first she'd heard about a furnace. The next morning Dad built Butch's coffin, and now she was digging his "final resting place," as she'd learned when she looked up synonyms for "grave." Butch often lay in the shade under the magnolia tree, so she knew he'd like staying here.

The hole was about two feet deep when she hit something that made a hard *thump,* not metallic this time. The suggested depth, according to "grave-digging" on Wikipedia, was four to five feet for a dog the size of Butch. The deeper she dug, the softer the soil had become, until she heard that *thump*.

Had her shovel bitten into a root? Dad warned that it might. Kneeling again, she scooped out soil with her hands until she found what she'd hit: not a tree root but a box.

Oh, please God let it not be someone else's dead pet.

Carefully, she brushed soil away until she revealed the entire top of the rectangular box. If it was an animal, it would have to be small, only a kitten or puppy, which made her think of Butch as a pup. What if a car had struck him down way back then? They wouldn't have grown up together and...

Tears crowded hotly behind her eyelids. She blinked hard, but they slid down her cheeks.

Maybe she should ask Dad to open the box.

The thought lay in her mind while she stared at the writing on the box top, *King Edward Imperial Cigars.* She was pretty sure no one would bury a box of cigars, but maybe it wasn't an animal at all. Maybe it was someone's buried treasure. There could be money or jewels or private letters. Now that she thought about it, only a dead bird or turtle would fit easily into a cigar box. She'd never had a turtle, and she didn't like birds. Not as pets, anyway. Too creepy, with their pecky beaks and quick beady black eyes. She knew a kid whose pet was a white rat, so she might find rat bones inside. It was possible, Betsy supposed, to love a rat or a turtle as much as she loved Butch, but the whole idea of it gave her a grubby feeling, like she wanted to wash her hands of more than just dirt. How did you snuggle up and watch TV with a bird or a turtle?

Those thoughts ran through her mind as she scooped out dirt and removed the box from the hole. Rat bones would not make her cry, so she set the box down and... *really quick*—opened it.

Whew! She dropped the lid and turned away. Whatever it was stank like rot.

She emptied her lungs then took a big gulp of fresh, clean air and held it as she opened the box again.

It was a cat.

Not dead, and not one that had ever been alive. It was a wooden cat, all proper and snooty on its haunches, the way she'd often seen cats sit. It didn't look like a figurine from the dollar store, more like someone had carved it by hand out of wood, blackish wood that didn't seem to be painted. Its eyes were tiny green crystals.

Betsy exhaled, then gently sniffed. The stink was gone, or at least going. Nothing in the box appeared to be rotted, and the cat was actually kind of pretty. Maybe Mom would like it for her curio cabinet. She had a collection of what she called her "oddities," interesting things she'd bought at garage sales and thrift stores. This cat certainly was odd. When Betsy turned it one way or the other, the cat seemed to continue looking at her, like those paintings in the museum where a person's eyes followed as you walked past. Maybe the green crystals played tricks in the sunlight. She put the cat aside, with the cigar box and the crucifix, and continued her work.

Why would anybody bury a cat figurine? Was it valuable? Had it been carved by someone famous? Or maybe the eyes were actually precious gems. Emeralds. If so, if it really was a treasure, why hadn't the owner come back to reclaim it?

Her parents bought their house six years ago, just before she entered first grade. They'd chosen the best school for their only daughter, Dad said, even before they looked for a house in the area. A year later, her brother Kyle was born.

Kyle was at Cub Scout camp for the summer. She was glad he didn't have to be here. Kyle loved Butch as much as she did.

So the cat must have been buried at least six years. Betsy wondered who had owned their house before them. Maybe she should find out. The real estate woman who sold it might know.

If Betsy could find the family who lived here, she'd ask if anyone had buried a cigar box under the magnolia tree. To make sure it was theirs, she could ask them what was in the box.

Seemed like a lot of trouble if it turned out to be a leftover clue from a treasure-hunt party, but it was something to think about, to pass the time while she finished digging Butch's gr... his final resting place before dog Heaven. Betsy wondered how long a dead person or a dead dog had to stay buried before ascending to meet God and the angels. Of course, some people went to the other place, but not Butch. He was a good dog, and he'd be waiting for her. Knowing she'd see him again gave her the first real smile she'd had all day.

Finished! Betsy stood back, stuck the shovel in the unturned ground and leaned on it to rest. The hole looked at least four feet deep and just right for the coffin to fit snuggly inside.

While Betsy washed up, Mom padded Butch's coffin with a small rug he liked to sleep on and Dad had laid him inside. Betsy tucked his favorite toy between his paws. Together, she and Dad carried him to the hole Betsy dug.

"Good job, Queenie. Perfect fit."

Mom joined them outside. They each said what they remembered best about Butch and wished him safely into God's hands, amen. Replacing the dirt took only a smidgen of the time it had taken to remove it.

"We're going out for dinner," Mom said. "I think we all need to get away for a while, but take your vitamins before we go."

Mom was a stickler for vitamins. They were look-alikes, she and Mom, both with chestnut hair, hazel eyes, and skinny—that's why the vitamin obsession. That night, they went to Betsy's favorite Italian restaurant. Calories galore, yum.

Later, after they were home and she was putting on her pj's, she remembered the things she'd found while digging. Sliding into flip-flops, she finished buttoning and went downstairs. Mom and Dad were watching TV, so she padded quietly out to the back porch. It was awfully dark out in the bushes. Maybe the cross and other things would be okay outside until morning.

When she started back upstairs, she heard a purring sound, felt something soft brush against her leg, then closed her eyes against a sudden spell of dizziness. A moment later, she opened them to find herself standing in the yard, staring down at two tiny two green lights in the grass. The cat?

Still dazed, she picked it up, along with the crucifix and cigar box. Her head cleared. She looked around, unsure how she'd gotten here from the porch. She didn't remember walking. Feeling a creepy nudge on the back of her neck, she rubbed it and returned to her bedroom, where she laid the items she dug up on her desk.

The cat sat gleaming at her. The green eyes were really pretty, but...strange.

Hastily, Betsy opened the cigar box, shoved the cat inside and placed the crucifix on top. Then she kicked off her flip-flops, damp from the dewy grass, wiped her feet on a dirty t-shirt she'd dropped on the floor, and climbed in bed.

Sleep came easily. It had been a long, sad, hard-working day. But recalling the words everyone said at Butch's funeral, she drew relaxing comfort into her lungs. Just as Butch's tail often thumped the floor when he was happy, Betsy's heart gently thumped with gladness that she had taken good care of him on his way to Heaven.

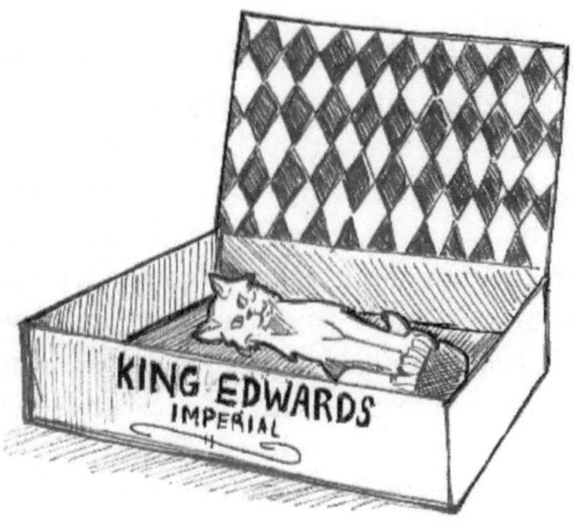

The next day, Saturday, was Mom's day to visit resale shops. Dad had to buy a new blade for the lawn mower, which meant he'd spend hours browsing through tools and fishing gear. They both asked Betsy to come along, but she begged off to do homework. She felt like all her sadness was buried right along with Butch, and she wanted to chill out. Play a video game.

When she went to get her phone, where her best games were stored, she saw little clumps of dirt on her desk near the cigar box. Her desk was the one spot she kept neat. Clothes might litter the floor, her dresser might be thick with dust, but Betsy wanted her desk clean.

She grabbed the crucifix off the cigar box. The silver was not shiny like Mom's silver tray, but it had a soft glow, and holding it gave her a warm feeling inside. It also had a few spots of soil, so she wiped it on her pajama pants before laying it on the desk.

"Cobwebs on the brain," Mom would say, when Betsy did something dorky. Last night must have been one of those cobwebby nights. Moving the dirty cigar box to the trash, she noticed some odd scribbles on top, worked into the design around the name. They were also on the sides and bottom.

Interesting but not important, and she had no use for a cigar box. She lifted the lid, though, and peered at the cat inside. Even canted sideways it seemed to be looking at her. Weird. Just the sort of oddity Mom would like, and someone had buried it, so it might be valuable.

After wiping her desk free of dirt clumps, she polished the top with the dust cloth she kept for cleaning her electronic tablet and phone. Then, leaving the box in the trash, she carried the cat to the bathroom to wipe clean before putting it on Mom's shelf. The wood felt nice, smooth but not slick. She liked the color, too, not jet black but what her art teacher would call "cool dark gray." Except for one white foot, which Betsy hadn't noticed before, probably because it was a hind foot and sort of tucked under the cat's body. Not exactly white, because the wood wasn't painted, but a pale wood color, maybe bleached by the sun. She wondered if the sculptor had picked that piece of wood because of its odd coloring or had bleached the foot with chemicals after it was carved.

Betsy wasn't particularly artsy. People she drew looked as stiff as cardboard, and her trees resembled popsicle sticks with green cotton tops, so she was amazed at what other kids in her class could do with colors and clay and stuff. This cat even had tiny whiskers, and the eyes weren't glued on top of the wood, as she first thought. They were set into little sockets carved in the wood.

Downstairs in the living room, Betsy studied the cabinet where Mom kept her curios. Wow, she had a lot. Lucky the shelves had a glass door or Mom would be dusting constantly. Betsy didn't see a single open space where the cat could sit without being squeezed against other items. Maybe she'd let Mom decide where to put it. Meanwhile, it could stay in her room.

In her bedroom again, she looked around. No way she'd waste her Saturday cleaning. The only uncluttered space besides her desk was the windowsill. While she didn't know much about cats, her grandma had a big yellow Tabby named Amber, and Amber liked to sit on top of the sofa just under the window.

Betsy placed the cat on the windowsill. She sort of liked it there, so if Mom didn't want it she'd keep if for herself. Hungry, she decided to get a snack. When she turned to go, a spot on her neck tingled. She rubbed it, glancing back at the cat, and got the weird notion it was watching her.

Girl you are creeping yourself out. She shrugged it off and laughed. *Get real.*

Four steps out the door, she remembered the silver cross. Dad had promised to make Butch's marker when he came home. Stepping back inside her room, her gaze went straight to the windowsill and the green-eyed cat staring back. She grabbed the crucifix, ran downstairs, out to Dad's shop and laid it on his workbench, where he was sure to find it. While eating her snack, cream cheese on cinnamon raisin bread, with milk to wash it down—Mom never bought sodas to drink at home—she flipped through Mom's magazine of collectibles. No hand-carved cats, but she did see an article about wood carvings, and some of them were blackish, mostly African masks. They didn't seem to be particularly valuable, unless they were ancient.

Upstairs again, she was lying on her bed deep in a game when she felt her eyelids getting heavy. Her bedroom was dim and cool, perfect for napping. Since Mom and Dad were both lazy shoppers, she'd have plenty of time for homework before they returned.

She shoved her phone under a pillow, pulled a soft blanket up to her chin and hoped Butch was as snug in his forever bed. If not for that dumbass drunk driver, Jason Clark...*was that his name?* His car and license plate were burned into her brain. It was Dad who confronted the driver and identified him to the police, but she'd posted his name online. She'd been too upset not to blast the unfairness of Butch's death all over the Internet, wanting the driver to pay for what he did. If not for Jason Drunkass Clark, Butch would be curled up beside her right now. It wasn't good Karma to be vindictive, but she couldn't shed the sharp sliver of resentment that had lodged in her chest. For the moment, though, she covered it with her comfy blanket so she could sleep.

Sleep never felt better than at Saturday naptime. She liked being alone in the quiet house, no one coaxing her to clean her room or rake leaves or...

A weight plopped onto her bed, jarring her. Drowsily, she felt the weight shift as if from foot to foot, moving closer, like Butch when he jumped up to watch her play videos, but it wasn't Butch. Butch was gone, Butch was...she dozed...then fell into deep slumber.

Betsy woke to her phone chiming, the room cloaked in storm shadows. Something heavy pressed on her chest. A whispery voice filled her ears.

You're mine, the voice said. *You're mine, you're mine,* or was it *meow*? No. *Mine, you're mine, you're*—over and over while something tickled Betsy's face.

PRETTY GREEN EYES

She lifted her eyelids and stared into brilliant green eyes. A huge gray cat, its face bigger than hers, its pink nose only a hair's breadth from her own, opened its mouth wide, teeth as sharp as needles. On its stinking breath came the whisper, *you're mine*.

Betsy yelped, pushed the blanket away and sat up all in one instant.

Nothing there. No cat.

Her phone was jangling. She peered at the clothes littering the floor around her bed and looked hard into the corners of her room.

Nothing. Just a stupid dream. A very *real* dream, very scary, but just a very stupid, *stupid, STUPID* dream.

She seized the phone. It was Mom. "Bets, were you napping?"

"No, yeah, sort of. What's up?"

"Your dad and I met for lunch when this rainstorm started and now we're flooded in. Are you okay? Did you eat?"

"Sure, I'm fine, and it's not raining all that hard here."

"Okay. The traffic is ridiculous, cars stalled in the street, SUVs pushing on through, but we plan to stay here until it's safe to drive. Don't forget your vitamins, and don't go out on your bike."

"I won't." Actually, that was exactly the thought crossing her mind. A fast bike ride might shake off the creepy mood caused by the dream.

After they disconnected, she went to the window to look out. The wooden cat sat there on the sill, all proper and snooty, staring at her. She pushed it to one side and looked down at the back yard. No flooding, just rain.

She gave the cat a puzzled glare then stepped back from the window. If she couldn't ride her bike, there was another way to shake off the dream. She punched up "Lane Boy" by 21 Pilots on her phone and bobbed her head and her hand to the beat. Tossing the phone on the bed, she shook the other hand, her arms, shoulders, head, butt, and started moving her feet. Not dancing, just shaking it off, shaking it down, shaking it out.

When the music stopped, she was breathing hard, wide awake and smiling. Her gaze fell on the wooden cat again. It was nothing. Just a wooden figure her brain had grabbed hold of to scare her out of her sorrow over Butch. She winked at it, snatched up her phone and danced downstairs for a little more game time before doing her boring homework.

Hitting a spot where the game became clunky and tedious, she noticed a message had come in. She tapped it open. *Jason Clark Cashes In—see video.*

"No way!" Betsy clicked on the link. "If that jerk's lawyer got him off—" Her throat tightened as she remembered the horrible *thunk* when the jerk's car hit Butch.

The video showed the same car, speeding down a neighborhood road then suddenly skidding, spinning and crashing into a humongous tree. The driver's side door popped open. The driver slumped forward on the crash bag. A closer view showed blood dripping from his mouth. Then the video cut to a stretcher being loaded aboard an ambulance. The boy's was face blocked by an EMS tech carrying the stretcher.

Betsy had seen enough to know it was indeed Jason Clark. She felt sick. Yes, she wanted him punished, but not like that.

Something bothered her about the video. She didn't really want to watch it again, but something bothered her and made her hit the play button. Silver car racing, skidding, spinning, crashing. A few seconds of wobbly silence as the person filming walked closer and the door swung open—*there!* A cat on the sidewalk. A gray cat with one white foot.

Betsy ran upstairs and flung open the door to her room.

The wooden cat sat on the windowsill just as before, its green eyes staring into her own.

Get a grip, girl! What you're thinking is nuts.

Betsy looked from the gray cat on the sill to the frozen video in her hand, where a gray cat with one white rear foot stood watching Jason Clark's auto accident.

She closed the door to her room and sat on the top stair, thinking.

***

By the time her parents returned, Betsy's homework was finished and the wooden cat was gone from the window sill. Betsy had dug a hole, not under the magnolia tree but on the far side of the yard, a small hole but deep.

She dropped the cat to the bottom. *You're mine. You're mine.*

Betsy started singing "Lane Boy" through gritted teeth to block out the whispers. She grabbed her shovel.

A pair of glittering green eyes swirled upward. *You're mine, you're mine, you're...*

Betsy filled the shovel with soil and—

...mine, You're...

—threw it into the hole—

...mine, you're mine, you're mine, you're mine... mine... mine... mine...

A car horn jarred her alert. Mom, honking to say they were home and to come help carry in their purchases.

How long had she stood there? Betsy shook herself, muttering, "Never mind, just fill in the freakin hole!"

She did, packing in every grain of dirt she could gather and stomping it down hard.

***

Later, as soon as Mom was busy in the kitchen and Dad went to his workshop, Betsy sat on the stairs, thinking. *Did I dig up a demon cat and bring it into our house? Or do I have a brain tumor?* She didn't know which would be worse.

She heard her dad sawing wood. The saw stopped and the drill started. She imagined him screwing pieces of Butch's marker together. *He's probably wondering why I'm not out there helping him.* She wanted to be, but that video and the whispers had her bummed. She wanted to ask Dad about it, show him the video and ask about the cat.

She didn't want him thinking she was nutso. Probably she *was* nutso.

When the carpentry sounds stopped, she ran out to see the finished marker. It looked great, a simple cross made of natural redwood that would last a long time, and the silver crucifix positioned at the center.

"We could have a nameplate engraved instead," Dad suggested.

Betsy shook her head. "I'll never forget Butch's name, and I like the idea of two crosses for double protection."

Dad cocked an eyebrow. "Protection from what?"

Right. From what exactly? She never lied to her father, but how could she admit being spooked by a feline wood carving? "You know, from zombie gophers and such."

"Of course. I've noticed them prowling our yard at night."

She hugged him, and together they set the marker. After dinner, with Mom cleaning the kitchen and Dad repairing the lawn mower, Betsy went to her room. She pulled the cigar box from her trash and studied the writing worked into the design. It appeared to be the same phrases, or a sentence, repeated on top, bottom and all four sides.

Carefully, she copied the words onto a sheet of paper. *Redimio meus inimicus thrice inter amo an ferrum manus manus. Is non permoveo vel reputo vel animadverto Ut vulnero mihi iam. Sic Mote Is Exsisto.* Then she carried the paper downstairs.

She knew without asking what Mom would say. "Betsy, is this your homework?" So she went out to the workshop.

"Dad, do you know what kind of language this is?"

"Hmmm. Looks like Latin. Where did you find it?"

"On an old cigar box." She told him about finding it in the hole she had dug for Butch, a foot or so beneath the silver crucifix, but didn't mention the cat. "Can you tell what it says?"

"Not a clue. Sorry, Bets. Is it important?"

"Probably not. I was just wondering."

"If it's Latin, surely someone at your school can translate it."

Off hand, Betsy couldn't think of a single teacher who might help her, but Dad had given her an idea. Didn't the Internet have online translators? *Duh.*

She typed the words into her tablet, but had to break it into sentences before the translator would tackle it, and wasn't certain how accurate the results were. They sort of made sense. *Bind my foe thrice around like an iron band. He cannot move or think or see to harm me now. Make it be so.*

That last phrase reminded her of something said by *Star Trek*'s Captain Picard. The other part convinced her she didn't have a brain tumor. Whoever put the cat figure in the cigar box had been serious about keeping it buried.

It wasn't bound "thrice" by anything visible, so it must be the words themselves that bound it, like an incantation.

***

After an ordinary Sunday at the grandparents' house for dinner and board games, Monday began like any normal school day. During a surprise math challenge, math being her best subject, Betsy threw out answers like corn popping. She went to lunch on a cloud amid high-fives and fist-bumps from her team.

Sharona, a girl from the opposing team, tripped Betsy while she was carrying her lunch tray. She didn't quite fall, but her dessert dish flew off the tray, landing face down on the floor.

"Oops!" Sharona's eyes and mouth grew round in mock surprise. "I guess even a math whiz can have two left feet."

Betsy let it pass. She and Sharona King had been besties in first grade but had grown apart after a third-grade spelling bee. Betsy was a good speller. Crappy in history and science, where she had to work hard for a B+, but reading, spelling and math were her sweet spots. Cleaning dessert goop off the floor, she found herself smiling at Sharona's petty payback.

Later that day, at volleyball practice, Betsy's height placed her close to the net, as usual, where she could spike the ball over for a sure point. Sharona played middle hitter, and this time, her aim was spot on. When Betsy jumped forward to set a ball, Sharona stepped in her path.

Betsy hit the floor in a painfully, awkward sprawl. Sharona was penalized, and Betsy had to go to the nurse. Just an ordinary day at school, until...

School was out. Betsy, headed to the bike rack, noticed everyone looking at their phones and rushing back toward the schoolhouse. She ran, too, to see what was happening.

In a fourth-floor window, Sharona sat with her legs dangling over the sill.

She was shaking her head as if frantically saying "no." Betsy couldn't see anyone with her, so who was she talking to?

Betsy's phone pinged with a text. It was from a school friend. "Nurse and science teach gone to help."

"No!" Sharona screamed. Her hands gripped the window sill.

To push herself off or to hang on? Betsy couldn't tell. "Don't do it, Sharona," she whispered. "Hang on, hang on, *please* hang on."

A wave of silent stillness spread through the crowd, as if noise might jar the girl off the ledge. In the quiet, Betsy could hear her cries, "No, no, I don't want to! No!"

Still shaking her head, Sharona plunged.

The science teacher appeared instantly in the window, reaching for her.

But too late.

***

By the time school security and counselors and the police let everyone leave, and Mom drove Betsy home, it was dark. No chance to do any digging outside.

She picked at her food. Mom and Dad didn't seem particularly hungry, either, and no one was talkative. After surprising Mom by helping to clean the kitchen, Betsy put on her pj's and buried her thoughts in her homework. Anything to take her mind off Sharona, *plummeting from the window...*

screaming all the way and... worst of all, the horrible sound when she hit the pavement.

Betsy shuddered, but the crying had finally stopped. No more tears. She would dig up the cat, put it back in the cigar box with the magic incantation and rebury it.

Cats were often said to be associated with witchcraft. *Familiars*, they were called, but what did that mean exactly? And how did it relate to a wooden cat?

Bind my foe thrice around...cannot move.. or harm me.... Was it possible that a witch or a wizard, had magically bound a witch's familiar, a *wicked* witch's *wicked* familiar inside the wooden cat? And those Latin words were on the cigar box to keep the familiar bound?

As a wooden cat, it *cannot move...or harm...*

But Betsy had taken it out of the box. Two people had died.

Maybe that was her fault. Maybe not. Maybe it was a brain tumor.

As she reached to turn off the bedside lamp, Betsy's gaze strayed to the window sill. She wished she'd never put the cat there. Silly, but at first glance she was certain it was back in the window. Her guilty conscience playing tricks? The magic words might only work for a witch or wizard, but she had to try. First thing tomorrow, she would set things right, set things back the way they were before her shovel found that cigar box.

Tomorrow wouldn't come, though, until she slept. The moon was shining in bright, and that always made her restless. She was hungry, too. "That's what happens when you don't eat your dinner," Mom would say.

Eyes determinedly closed, Betsy turned on her side and tucked the covers under her chin. In some stories, a witch could exchange bodies with a familiar. The witch could become a cat. Could it work the other way around, could the cat become a person? And was the wicked familiar-cat getting stronger the longer it was outside the cigar box?

Betsy turned on her other side. Her stomach felt absolutely, totally empty. A small bowl of cereal, and she would probably go right to sleep.

Quietly, she crept down to the kitchen, poured a bowl of Cheerios, added milk and leaned against the kitchen counter to eat it.

After only a few bites she felt better, sleepier. She put her elbows on the counter and took a last bite, closing her eyes. What a horrible, horrible week this had been. No wonder her body had gotten its eating and sleeping cues mixed up.

Mine.

Betsy's eyes popped open. She jumped back from the kitchen counter, where a cat was lapping at her milk. A gray cat with one white foot. When Betsy jumped, the milk had sloshed out of the bowl. Now the cat was staring at her with bright green eyes.

Betsy's eyelids popped open. She was in bed, lying on her side, covers tucked under her chin. She had dreamed it, all of it, but it seemed so real. She could taste the cereal, and she felt not at all hungry.

She pulled her blanket up and curled into a ball beneath it. After a long while, she fell asleep.

When morning came, Betsy caught her bottom lip between her teeth and bit down hard.

"Ow!" But she laughed, because the pain was a good sign. Somewhere she'd read that you don't feel pain in your nightmares, so she must be awake.

Her mouth tasted as if she hadn't brushed her teeth before bed. She went to the bathroom and took care of business. On the way out, her gaze went to the windowsill.

"No! No, no no, no no—" Already across the room, she snatched up the cat, squeezed it in both hands, wishing she could crush it, and glared into its freakish green eyes, hating it. "You can't be here. You're buried!"

You're mine.

Pretty Green Eyes

She was not asleep this time, couldn't be because she'd felt the pain of biting her lip. She knew she had brushed her teeth and emptied her bladder.

She could feel the solid substance of the cat figurine in her hands, the ears, the tail, the smooth, hand-carved wood. She could feel the warmth of the sun coming through the window, see the gleam of sunlight on the crystal eyes. She was definitely awake.

The sun felt warm on her skin. Soothing. The cat's wooden body was pleasant to touch, comforting to hold. Its pretty green eyes were gentle and calming to look at. The pretty green color spread into the sunlight falling on the window sill, on Betsy's hand and arm, on her pajamas, spread until it tinted her entire room green.

When Mom called Betsy down to breakfast, she set the cat back on the window sill. It looked good there.

She smiled and decided to keep it there.

"Don't forget your vitamins," Mom said, when they sat down to breakfast. She placed a capsule beside everybody's plate. "Betsy, I think this new brand is working for you better than for any of us. You look chipper this morning. Your skin looks clear and soft, and your eyes look...greener than usual."

"I feel good, too," Betsy said, sipping her milk. And it was true, she felt so good she could practically purr.

About the Author

A visual and literary creative, **Chris Rogers** began her journey as a graphic designer. Corporate and commercial promotions occupied most of her creative energy during those early years, but Rogers' adventurous spirit led her into diverse avenues where she designed personalized glassware, ceramic tile, and the launch issue of a national magazine.

With the advent of computerized graphics and an economic downturn, she was faced with a difficult choice: either learn this new electronic design tool or choose a new career. She began looking at what that new career might be – writing and illustrating children's books? Travel writing and photography? She tried her hand at each, and sold her photo-illustrated articles to regional and national publications, but before she was fully committed in any direction, a fire gutted her studio.

After salvaging a single drawing table from the ruins, she continued creating marketing materials for clients while seeking a new path in the literary world. Many rejections later, her stories began to win awards. A major publisher produced her suspense novels in print, electronic, and audio formats. Lauded by fans and critics, the books were translated into three languages, and the series was optioned for film.

While continuing to explore the literary venue, Chris inevitably embraced the creative form of paint on canvas, which allows her narrative flair and graphic origins to unfold in unison.

While creating new canvases, she also participates in the design of her book covers. Her paintings can be found in private and corporate collections.

Pretty Polly

By Curt Locklear

PRETTY POLLY

THE COOL MIST AND fog settled about the stable where Willie waited. Luther lay below a ragged bush, in hiding, studying him. The stable was a shabby railed pen with a meager cedar shake roof. Willie stood inside, peering into a gray smudge of fog. Sometimes, wisps of breeze revealed the dense, new-growth pine trees a few dozen yards away. He wiped the mist wetness from his face with a pitiful kerchief.

Luther, lying still as a tombstone, surveyed his nemesis and only friend.

Willie's angular face was clean-shaven, like always, and his youthful vigor exuded from him. He had pomaded his pompadour. His arms and shoulders, built hard and large from his lumber cutting job, bulged against a soiled plaid shirt. The shirt missed buttons. Mud splattered his pants and boots.

When Luther shifted a little in his hiding place, Willie's golden brown eyes rolled gradually in that direction like a crocodile sensing prey.

Luther came up from behind the ragged bush into a crouch. His beggarly suit was covered with mud and dead leaves. Hey, Willie, he said.

Willie said nothing.

-Did you see me there watchin' ya?

-Saw ya hours ago.

-I ain't been here but fifteen minutes.

-I heard your mind thinkin' bout it.

No sound, save a tiny bird twittering, and little dead leaves toppling though the branches of post oaks and pines.

Luther rose, brushed off his clothes. He wished he hadn't wasted his time hiding. He tried to cogitate how Willie could hear his mind and concluded that Willie was full of it. He strode up beside Willie and leaned against the rail opposite him a few feet down. –What ya doin'?

Willie's eyes darted at him. He said nothing.

-You're lookin' for Polly, Luther said. - This is her dead husband's stable and her horse, and she lives over yonder in her dead husband's house.

Willie fixed his eyes on Luther.

-You aim to kill her?

-Now why would I do that, Luther?

-Well, you said if you can't have her, ain't no man gonna.

-Figure o' speech.

-I dunno.

-Shut your yap. Willie paused. –You know those switchbacks up the mountain?

-Yeah, I do.

-A man'd fall off there if he wasn't careful.

-What do ya mean by that?

Willie stared into the grey nothingness. He stuck a straw in his lips.

In the shadows of the stable, Polly's grey plow horse half-slept in its stall, tiny gnats bothering its weary eyes. Its tail swatted flies that zipped from the piles of manure to the shivering hide of the horse, then to harass Luther's ears. He swatted at them.

Luther bit his lip. –You make any whiskey last night? he asked. He was thin as a walking cane and balding, and his greying hair stuck out like tangled cobwebs. It was hard to tell his skin color. Some would say lavender, others would say jaundiced peach. His back had an S curve in it that made his walk a'kilter. He knew his place in this forlorn mountain society. He was one of the offscourings.

-You want whiskey, Luther? Willie bit at a torn fingernail.

-That I do. Got a silver watch here to pay.

-Revenoors.

-What?

-Revenoors sneakin' around. Pokin' around.

Luther sighed, stuck his hand in his jacket pocket, fingering the watch he'd pilfered off a dying woman's vanity. –Can't make no money. No jobs. This depression. Roosevelt said he'd fix things. Ain't seen it. Probably takin' care of all his northern buddies. Making us Texans wait 'til last.

Willie set his foot down from the rail, unbuttoned his pants' front and relieved himself on Luther's breeches.

Luther jumped back. –Why'd ya do that, you..?

-Say it, Luther. You think I'm a bastard!

Luther shook his pants leg and grabbed straw from the ground to wipe off the piss. Willie finished and re-buttoned his pants.

Luther looked up. - I believe you could kill a man.

-Never could.

No more words, nothing but the sound of the flies buzzing and the horse's tail swatting. The fog became a heavy layer, like a sky below the sky. Luther moved under the roof now.

In a little while, a sudden, stiff breeze blew, and the sun melted the fog so Luther could see through the gray curtain.

-Polly's comin'. I hear her mind, Willie said.

Luther looked long at Willie. –Too bad about her husband up and shootin' his self. He thought she was bein' untrue.

-Untrue?

-You know. He saw her traipsin' about with Widow Hillary's boy. He didn't know no better. He shoulda never married a girl that pretty. That's askin' for trouble.

Willie spit.

Luther spit. Some of the spittle dribbled down his grizzled beard. He wiped it with his sleeve. He looked at the bubbly streak on the cloth.

Willie held Luther's wrist to his nose. –You smell like rotten leaves and stale booze, worse than the manure odor. Did you see him traipsin' around with the widow's boy, Luther?

-No, but the widow told me she was seein' her boy.

-And you believed her? The lyingest bitch in the county, in

the nation. I would never give Widow Hillary my ear to listen to because sure enough she'd fill it with yarns. Remember how she said she was ridin' in Fort Worth, and the mob was firin' tommy gun bullets all around her. Lie. Lie. Then her friend who was with her the whole time told the truth that the whole thing never happened. But Widow Hillary's excuse was she was tired. Polly's husband just wasn't right in the head.

Luther couldn't remember when he'd heard Willie say such a string of sentences all at one time. He clucked his whiskey-dry tongue, pulled a licorice twist from his pocket and chewed on it.

Then there was a fluttering at the lower branches of the young pines, whispering. The branches parted like a vessel cleaving the water. Luther and Willie could see a feminine arm and the hem of a skirt, but the upper branches hid the identity. Willie looked up to the sky, his face reverent in appearance. Then Polly appeared, decked out in a flouncy pastel blouse and a tan, simple skirt. Pausing in the clearing, she put her hands behind her back, ducked her head, blushing. A hint of gardenias wafted over to them.

–Hey, Polly, Willie said. You're lookin' mighty pretty today.

-Why thank you, she replied, all excessive demure drawl.

-C'mere. Willie beckoned with two curled fingers.

-Ok. She skipped forward, her hands grabbed onto her skirt, swishing it back and forth.

She stopped just past arm's length, twirled a finger in her long auburn hair.

Polly was, in Luther's estimation, as pretty a woman as ever there'd been since Eve. She had an hourglass shape, heavy in the bosom, soft brown hair that hung past her shoulders, a bright cheerful face with a petite nose and large doe eyes. He thought Willie better look out.

She'll put a love spell on him, like she did to her dead husband.

Luther thought she didn't look a bit for sorrow over the death of her husband that died but a month ago. He asked her – Been to Johnnie's grave?

Polly scowled at him. - You stinkin' piece of shit. Why'd you ask that? The flush was fierce red on her cheeks.

-Ain't you got somethin' to do, Willie said to Luther.

-Yeah, yeah. I'm gone. Luther slipped under the rail and headed off. Once he was deep enough into the woods, he ducked behind a thick pine trunk, listening.

-You miss me much, Willie? Polly drawled.

-Sure enough. I like your company. Say, I soaked some tobacco leaves in sorghum water, dried 'em out, set 'em in the smoke house. I know you don't chaw, but would you like to see?

Luther thought that an odd way of courting a girl.

-Sure, but not right now, Polly said.

Luther's hiding spot afforded him a view of Polly's back. He found himself observing how her shoulder blades curved the fabric of her blouse and how her tresses lightly fell down between them to the small of her back.

Polly finally stepped closer to Willie. She lifted her arm and stroked his cheek ever so tenderly. –You have nice eyes.

Luther heard it clear as a bell. He couldn't agree with her estimation because he'd never seen anything but deceit and loathing in Willie's eyes.

Where she stood now, Luther couldn't see Willie, except his forehead and hair. He heard some shuffling and Willie clearing his throat and the soft rustling of cloth against cloth. He saw Willie put his arms around Polly. His hands slid down her back to rest on her buttocks.

Luther coughed. He didn't mean to. Both Willie and Polly turned their heads.

-Got to go, Polly said. See you at the barn dance. Don't forget.

-I won't, Willie called.

Then Polly flitted away to her house, passing close to where Luther hid. After she was gone, Willie commanded— Come out, Luther.

Luther marched forward, doing a goose step like the German soldiers in a photograph in an Atlanta newspaper he'd looked at. –Takin' her to the dance?

-Naw. She's still in mourning. Wouldn't look right. I'll meet her there.

-Just because you kissed her, don't make her yours.

-Hell, it don't. Any man try somethin', I'll punish him.

Willie beat his fist into his palm. –Don't you say nothin'. I mean it. Luther backed away, then turned into the forest.

The rain came in early evening, just enough to hide the harvest moon and make the low spots in the road a sloppy, sucking mess. In the mizzling rain, Luther trod up the steep road out of town and looked like a lame jack rabbit hopping the muddy holes. He knew old Uncle Pen would be sawing on his fiddle. No one could play like that man. He was no one's uncle, but all the folks called him that. Even from a distance, Luther heard the music floating out and banking back and forth against the hillsides, then floating up into the hidden early stars. Uncle Pen's fiddle sang, and sometimes seemed to talk.

Luther snapped his fingers in rhythm. He considered that there would likely be spiked punch, and his mouth watered. He rounded the turn and beheld the barn. Lanterns all around burned like daylight. He stopped, brushed dust from his jacket. He yanked a pine branch from a tree and rubbed the branch in his armpits, then sniffed. Satisfied, he strode lazily past the cars and pickups and a dozen saddled horses, then through the barn door.

The couples were dancing to "Soldier's Joy" with abandon. Up in the loft, Uncle Pen beat his bow on his fiddle, a young fellow chomped on a harmonica, and a drummer banged his hardest on a snare and cymbal. The couples whirled and swung like they'd never have another chance to dance in their lives. Their clothes were sweaty, their brows wet.

A few individuals sat on hay bales and railback chairs, tapping their feet and smiling.

Others stood drinking cups of punch. Luther estimated about forty folks had alighted from miles around like June bugs round a porch light.

Luther cared not a whit about dancing, and he ached to sip on the punch, but he held himself steady, made a point to gaze around and smile at a few individuals. When they saw him, they made sour faces and turned their heads. The band finished the piece, and ancient Uncle Pen announced in a creaky voice a short break. The band members grabbed beer bottles and chugged away. Luther decided he would see where they stashed their beer.

His eyes dropped below the loft and he saw Willie leaning against a support post conversing with Polly, seated on a bale. His arms were sailing around like he was telling her of some exploit, and she was giggling. Just then, Rueben Eddle walked up, thumbs in his pants loops and addressed Polly. Willie stiffened like an iron rod. Polly smiled at Rueben. Willie scowled at her, but she looked to be talking kindly to Rueben. He took hold of her hand and kissed it. Willie came forward, his face contorted fierce, and pushed Rueben's shoulder. Rueben ignored Willie and turned slowly away, a smirk on his face. Luther wished he could have heard what was said.

He did hear Polly call out sweetly - Goodbye, Rueben. Tell your mama 'hey'!

Willie took hold of her arm and spun her around on the hay bale, but she smiled at him and stroked his arms. In a moment, he was smiling.

Luther made his way methodically to the punch table. He saw the whiskey jug sitting underneath the table and kicked it, could tell it was empty. He dipped the ladle in the punch bowl, poured himself a full cup, his hands trembling. In two minutes, he had slurped four cups. He wiped his mouth with his sleeve, said ahhhh.

The band came back and began a slow waltz. Luther watched Willie lead Polly onto the dance area. Other couples joined them. Willie and Polly didn't move much, just a slow sway, their foreheads touching, arms tight around each other. Luther watched the reactions of the other couples when they passed the lovers. Most looked perturbed.

Hiram Floyd sauntered up and tapped Willie on the shoulder. Before Willie could respond, Hiram, big as an ox, invaded his space and danced Polly away in clumsy steps. Willie's face burned red, his fists clenching and un-clenching.

The waltz ended with Willie alone in the middle of the floor. He stormed outside. In a moment, Polly skipped quickly after him and caught him. The rain had stopped, and she put her arms around his waist. He resisted. Finally, she tugged him inside. She was smiling. Willie looked embarrassed in Luther's estimation.

Cord Jones, the minister's son, walked by them. He called to Polly- You're lookin' mighty pretty tonight, Mrs. Cory. – calling her by her married name.

She smiled. -Come by the house sometime – she said - and bring your pa.

Willie seemed to show little emotion. He nodded at the reverend's son, then ducked his head down, mumbling.

Polly looked abashedly at him. Willie turned his back to her. She rubbed his back with both hands.

The alcohol was working its way on Luther's brain. Suddenly, he said - Hope Willie don't kill one of them boys.

-What'd you say? Old Man Sample said, huffing.

-Nothin'

-I heard you. What'd you mean about Willie?

-Nothin'. Willie drew another cup of the punch, poured it down his throat and walked quickly away.

Old man Sample hollered - What'd you mean about Willie?

Luther rushed out past Willie and Polly still at the barn door. As he passed, he said -Don't act jealous, Willie.

The band's song ended and for a split moment, the barn was quiet, and in that vacuum of sound, Willie bellowed out -I'll be jealous if I want to.

Everyone turned and gawked at Willie. He saw them staring at him and he pivoted around and plowed like a bear out into the forest. Polly ran after him for a while, but she stopped when he would not turn. He vanished into the dense trees.

Polly trod slowly back and passed Luther, standing with his head down. - My mind is to marry that man, Luther – she said. - I love him to death.

It was dark now, and Luther chose to cut his losses and find his way home in the dark. He pulled a rough, roach-chewed, tallow candle from his pocket, lit it, and held the thing in one hand, cupping the flame with his other. Luther wondered what Uncle Pen's fiddle was saying.

The old fiddler had commenced playing the sprightly "Georgia Rose," but, to Luther, it sounded a weary, melancholy rendition. In a few yards, he was out of earshot.

The next day, Willie didn't go to the logging company. He told a fellow worker to tell the shift boss he was sick. Luther guessed Willie was home and climbed the long hill up to his cabin, wanting whiskey.

He heard Willie inside, pots and pans clattering, and a chair scraping the floor. He entered. -Whiskey? He asked.

Willie was at the stove, frying an egg. He shook his head no.

Luther's face fell. He shuffled across the floor, sat by the table and looked at Willie's back. Luther smelled the egg burning.

-Egg's done, Luther said.

Willie shoved the smoking pan to the back of the stove with a clang. He closed the stove damper and sat next to Luther, then buried his face in his palms.

For a long moment, the only sound was the clock ticking. Luther said - Polly wants to marry you.

-I know she does. Willie never raised his head.

He got up abruptly and raged outside with Luther on his heels. He went to his shed where he kept his still and pulled out a spade, slung it over his shoulder and marched out into the forest.

-Hope you ain't gonna wail on some man with that shovel! Luther called after him.

Luther watched him go, then he slunk back into the shed, grabbed a tin cup from a nail and sought to gather any leavings from the sour mash in an oak half barrel. He scraped and scraped and only managed a few sips from the tub. He heaved a sigh, sat back and looked at his hands trembling. In a moment, he fell asleep seated on the floor and propped against the tub.

He awoke when Willie clumped in and hung up his shovel. Luther watched him grab his ax. - Hey! Luther said.

-I can hear her thoughts, Luther.

-What'd ya mean?

-Just what I said. I can hear Polly thinkin'. She's thinkin' about other men.

-She told me she wanted to marry you. Luther stood.

Willie snuffed. You need a bath, Luther. You stink like a privy.

Willie walked out with his ax. Luther pulled the watch he'd stolen from his pocket. - Think I'll buy a hot bath at the hotel.

Luther traded the watch for a bath and to have his clothes washed. He shaved. When he donned the fresher clothes, he took his sharp pocket knife and cut off some of his long hair. He slathered his hair with perfumed pomade. When he looked in the hotel hall mirror, he felt right proud. He sashayed out into the bright day and spied, across the way, Polly leaving the general store and loading a heavy flour sack on her wagon. He scanned the town and saw folks around the stores and boardwalk. Sheriff Cordell was turning the crank of an old Model T.

Polly accidentally whacked her elbow on the wagon sideboard. She hollered. Five men, young and old, and including Sheriff Cordell, rushed to come to her aid. She waved them off. Luther snickered at the men, each of them so keen to be near her, all of them blushing and pulling off their hats to say - how do, Mrs. Cory?

When he saw old man Sample return to his wife and her swatting him on the arm, he laughed out loud. He walked over to Polly when she climbed to the wagon seat. -Hey, Polly - he said.

-What you want, you old peckerwood?

-Just sayin' hey. Wanted to let you know that Willie thinks about you all the time. Would you think me unkind to ask you to tell me your mind?

Polly looked long into the sky. -My mind is to marry him and never to part. - She paused. -The first time I saw him, he wounded my heart. All I think about is Willie. He has my devotion to my dying day.

-And you have his. I'll be on my way.

She let out a long sigh. - Sorry I called you peckerwood.

She shook the reins, and the horse pulled the wagon out of town.

Luther suddenly realized it was Saturday and he was late to open his sharpening shop. When he got there, a line had formed. All the lumberjacks, the farmers, housewives and even a few businessmen needed their implements sharpened. He unlocked the door of his shaky, leaning shack and took in each man or woman one at a time and sharpened the ax or hoe or shears or knife on his grindstone. They each paid him two cents.

When he looked up for the last customer, he stared into Willie's face. Luther knew Willie always shaved, but he wasn't shaved now.

-Gimme your ax, Willie, I'll have it sharp as a widow's tongue in no time.

-Don't need my ax sharpened. He held out a long dagger knife with a pearl handle. Luther gently lifted the dagger from Willie's hands and laid it across his grindstone –Where'd ya get this fine instrument?

-A bum passin' through. He sold it to me for fifty cents.

Luther had the dagger sharp as a whistle in but two minutes. -Ain't no charge, Willie.

-Thanks, Luther.

-What ya plannin' to do with that pretty thing?

-Oh, nothin' special. Just caught my eye. He turned and walked slowly back to his green-eyed stud-horse he called Tennessee. He didn't mount the ancient horse, but led it. Luther could tell the limping animal had a swelling in the hock joint and suspected a bone spavin.

Willie said - Hope he don't kill no one with that knife.

A week later, Luther saw Polly and Willie eating dinner in the town's only café. Willie was smiling, and she was giggling to beat the band. Luther felt good for that. He also thought that this would be a propitious opportunity to ask Willie for a bottle. He wanted to say that Willie was the finest gentleman and Polly was the sweetest lady on the green earth. When he came in and said – Hey - he got tongue-tangled.

The two laughed at him.

-Another time, - Willie said, and waved him away.

Luther slunk off and headed up into the dark woods beyond the town to locate another fellow's still, hidden halfway up the mountain. It wasn't long before he was lost. He gave up and sat down hard against a pine tree trunk. He saw a running stream nearby but the idea of drinking water made him ill. He set to singing a little Irish drinking ditty he'd learned, one with suggestive words and commentary. He stared up at the stars. -Millions, he said.

In a little while, he felt too weary to search any further for the still or for the way home, so he brushed together a pile of pine needles and reclined. He was soon asleep. He thought he was awake in the earliest pearl gray morning light and everything seemed to be twirling. He believed he saw a large vulture circling, then he thought he saw Willie striding quickly along the stream bed carrying that shovel again. Before he could call out, the vision was gone.

The sun was full up when Luther awakened with a start. He heard voices. Willie's and Polly's. Sure enough. He looked down toward the stream, and there was Willie walking at a fixed pace, and Polly followed behind singing a little hymn, then she called out some words to Willie who answered her back friendly but firm-like. In a moment, they had vanished into the trees. He decided to follow. Maybe Willie had a new hiding place for his still.

The lovers' voices carried lightly like birds chittering. Polly sounded happy, Willie not so much. Willie called out to Polly - before we get married, some pleasure we'll find.

It occurred to Luther that maybe they were going to a secret place to make love, and fancying himself a stealthy spy, he might catch a glimpse of Polly naked. He hastened along, but his wobbling legs carried him zig-zag, and soon their voices had drifted to nothing.

-Ain't givin' up, he said. He forced himself to keep moving and when he ambled down an incline to a little clearing, he almost stumbled over Willie's horse - dead. The animal, still tethered by a heavy rope to a tree, had been stabbed through the chest and had bled out. The blistering heat brought with it a suffocating smell that stung his eyes and left the horse stiff as a board. Flies had already laid eggs in the eyes, and maggots crawled about its face and the torn wound. The smell was foul. Luther almost blacked out from the stench. He took one more quick look, then stumbled away.

- So that's what Luther wanted with that dagger. Durn fool. The vet woulda put the horse down for two dollars. It's a shame.

Luther's path was taking him down a steep incline, and he felt glad to be away from the dead horse. Then he heard their voices clear as an orchestra playing.

-I'm afraid of your ways, Willie, Polly said. - Why, did you bring me out here?

Luther ducked down, then slithered under a low-slung bush. He wanted a peek. In a moment, he had an excellent view of Willie and Polly in a shady meadow.

Polly was weeping. - I said, Willie, why did you take me out here?

-To show you this. Willie stepped to a dirty tarp on the ground and pitched it off, revealing a rectangular hole. The spade lay to the side.

Luther felt perplexed, and he saw the puzzlement, then dismay, then the horror in Polly's face.

-What do you intend to do, my love? Polly asked.

Willie took a firm hold of her arm. – I intend to end your thinkin' about other men. If I can't have you, ain't nobody gonna.

-But you do have me, Willie. Polly's voice was remorseful.

-I hear your talkin' to other men day and night. It's ending now.

-When did you hear me talkin' to other men? She sounded shredded into pieces. - I ain't never talkin' to anyone unless you're with me.

Willie pulled her to the edge of the open grave.

-Please, Willie, Polly begged.

-At dinner last night, I heard you thinkin' 'bout Johnny Cory.

- Johnny, my husband, is dead. Why would you think I could talk to him? How do you hear my thoughts?

-It don't matter how. I hear 'em. You're past reputation is causin' me horrible grief.

He pulled the long dagger from his belt, grabbed her by the waist with his free hand.

Luther saw it all like it was in slow motion. Polly knelt down pleading for her life. –Let me be a single girl if I can't be your wife.

Willie ripped off her shirt and cut her bra loose with the dagger, revealing her bosom as white as any snow. Then he stabbed her through the heart, and the blood overflowed. Polly let out a little guttural sound then toppled over.

Luther gasped, but did not utter a word.

Willie looked in Luther's direction, but he scanned too high and didn't see his hiding place.

In a moment, Willie gently picked up Polly's lifeless body and lay it in the shallow grave, then methodically he shoveled dirt into the hole until it was a low mound. He tossed the shovel like a javelin as hard as he could throw it.

Luther rose quiet as a mouse. Willie stood gazing off towards the low hills. Then he began batting his ears again and again. – No! No!- he railed. -Stop thinkin'! You're dead! Polly, stop it!

Luther was about to speak, though he feared Willie and the bloody dagger lying on the ground. He sneaked forward, picked up the weapon. Willie turned. When he saw Luther, he ran full on toward town.

Luther took after him. Up and down the hills, he could hear Willie wailing and wailing, so piteous a sound he'd never heard.

When Luther made it to town, he saw Willie, all animated like a marionette, talking to Sheriff Cordell. Suddenly, the sheriff grabbed Willie, handcuffed him and shoved him down on the boardwalk. The deputy walked up.

–Don't take your eyes off him! Sheriff Cordell said, then took hold of the arm of Hiram Floyd who was standing there gawking. The sheriff shouted - Come with me!

The two headed into the woods in the direction Willie was pointing.

Luther, the bloody dagger still in his hand, came up. - Here's your knife, Willie.

Willie never lifted his head. Luther shrugged, then handed the dagger to the deputy who gave a quizzical look.

-That's mine, Willie said.

Luther was walking away, as dazed as he'd ever been when he was drunk. He heard Willie call after him - Luther, I killed pretty Polly! I'm tryin' to get away.

Luther turned. –From her thoughts?

-Yes.

-God help you.

Luther went to the hotel mirror and stared at himself for a long time. He swore then and there he'd quit drinking, and he did. By and by, the lumber company foreman gave him a job cleaning out the office and taking messages out to the crews.

A month or so later, Uncle Pen hung up his fiddle and bow and took to his bed, pale as parchment. Luther sat for days at his bedside. When Uncle Pen asked Luther if he'd be a pallbearer at his funeral, Luther said - I will.

ABOUT THE AUTHOR

Curt Locklear is a published novelist. He has won awards for short stories. He is also an accomplished banjo and guitar musician. In the Texas PBS series, "The Daytripper with Chet Garner," the banjo picking at the beginning was conceived and performed by Mr. Locklear.

A retired educator, Mr. Locklear has taught English, History and Journalism. He even composed the Alma Mater school songs for four schools.

Asunder, A Novel of the Civil War is on Amazon.

Connect with Curt on Facebook

E-mail: curt@curtlocklearauthor.com

Pretty Polly is derived from an old time country song. Look carefully and see references to the songs sprinkled throughout the story.

Lessons of Tradition

By Angela Carpenter Hunsaker

LESSONS OF TRADITION

THE JOURNEY TO GRANNY Fisher's for Thanksgiving began with us all piling into the car and heading toward Baytown, Texas. I was a child peering out of the backseat window to catch a glimpse of landmarks that were familiar.

The "Spaghetti Bowl" was one landmark. It was a term we created to describe the jumbled ribbons of highway that intersected on the way to her house.

The next landmark was the old abandoned houseboat, which sat in a field. To pass the time, we would invent stories of the wealthy families who may have once inhabited it.

Lastly, we would see the neon Anheuser-Busch sign, which meant we were almost there.

After finally arriving and ringing the doorbell, we could hear Granny's laughter as she ran to answer the door. Some would say her laughter was more of a cackle, but it was a song to my ears. After opening the door, she would smother us in hugs and kisses, each of us feigning irritation, but we all loved her affection.

Entering her home, the mouth-watering aroma of her unique turkey and dressing wafted lazily toward the swirled textured ceilings. On the kitchen counter sat her "Aunt Jemima" cookie jar, which, in her era was not racist; it was just a down-home symbol. I just saw it as where to get the cookies.

Adjoining the kitchen was the breakfast nook, where there was a dinette table and a dressed-up card table, which were the 'kids tables', where my brother, sister, cousins, and me would be seated. In the dining room was the coveted 'adult table', set with Granny's finest china and a Chantilly lace tablecloth. This was a table at which I would never sit.

As I matured from a child to a teenager, I began to resent taking the trip to Baytown for Thanksgiving. It was a major imposition on my time. I had friends who invited me to celebrate the holiday with their families. Why was I chained to this tradition? I was very busy and had better things to do. It was boring. There was nothing to do there. I should've been allowed to experience other people's version of Thanksgiving.

As a result of several years of complaining, I managed to convince my mother to allow me to make other plans in 1979, the year I turned 17. I reveled in my manipulation of my mother, and felt liberated from the ho-hum familiarity of my grandmother's house.

I soon discovered that I was an outsider at my friend's house. I was an onlooker into someone else's life, and missed my family's familiar traditions.

The next Thanksgiving, I was secretly looking forward to visiting my grandmother, and surprised my mother by my lack of protest. But three weeks before Thanksgiving that year, my treasured Granny died suddenly of a massive heart attack in her home—the home where I now know my heart lived.

My family was instantly fragmented. The blur of a funeral and memorial service, my inconsolable mother, and everyone's great despair all contributed to the complete confusion of that holiday season. We could not find a way to deal with our loss together.

After my grandmother's funeral, everyone seemed to scatter and withdraw into his or her individual worlds. I ended up having Thanksgiving dinner that year in a dirty, mouse-infested punk rock bar, which a friend managed. The people gathered there were all misfits. Each of these people had no family celebration. These people were lost, as I was. I was, tragically, now one of them. They did not have family who really missed them, who really needed to be with them.

I realized how fortunate I was to be included in my family's "boring" tradition. I missed something for which I had never been grateful. Things that once seem mundane now took on a whole new meaning. Just to see those tacky ceramic goldfish in my grandmother's bathroom one more time. To play just one more game of touch football in the field beside her house. To act out just one more silly pantomime for my uncle's 8mm camera. To hear Granny's footsteps running toward the front door. The absence of all these feelings and experiences made my senses slightly dimmer, for a time.

But life goes on, and my grandmother instilled wonderful memories. True, there is no longer Thanksgiving celebrated with my late grandmother, but a new tradition has begun. For the record, I now sit at my throne at the 'adult table', and my own daughter, my niece and my nephews probably hate my tacky ceramic frog.

About the Author

Angela Carpenter Hunsaker was a prolific letter writer. She had 3 letters to the editor published in the Houston Post in the 80's. Angie always felt the need to write letters of praise whenever she received great customer service and letters of criticism whenever she didn't. She even wrote the Chief of Police, Lee Brown, whenever two patrol officers helped the then 20 something Angie, find her lost car keys. The letter was so compelling that Chief Brown responded personally, commended the officers, and put her letter into each of their files.

These stories, as submitted to the Houston Writers House, represent and older and wiser Angie reflecting on long ago childhood memories.

Angie was funnier, smarter, and more talented than most. She ran head-long into life when she was young, and, like a shooting star, she shown bright and dimmed too quickly, leaving us to try to go on without her. We will miss her. She passed away in 2016 and these are the memories she leaves behind.

Gracie's Story

By Peggy Stautberg

GRACIE'S STORY

THEY SAY YOU CAN look back at your life and discern an invisible dividing line—a seminal event that you point to with certainty and say, Yes—*that's* what happened. That's when the world started spinning around in a different direction.

For me, it was school, for my entrance into school coincided exactly with the ending of my family's happiness. That does sound a bit melodramatic, I know. But from around that time on, I was no longer cocooned. School pulled me loose. Over time, it forced me to look at my family the way a stranger might. I slowly came to see myself as a sort of exposed beam on the ceiling of the family home. I was the observer, taking it all in as my family's drama played out. For a long time, I just didn't understand how to reconcile the two worlds. The "normal" world around me, outside my home, seemed to speak in whispers. I, too, felt like a whisper. I spoke very softly back then, and mostly only when first addressed by someone else. I felt safer that way.

Before everything changed, our house near Texas City—my childhood home—was the best one we'd ever had because, as I've said, we were still happy. Mama's spells weren't so bad back then. And my father mostly did things right, so their constant arguing wasn't yet the norm.

Our "shantytown" as Mama jokingly called it, which irritated Daddy quite a bit, had been built on the outskirts of Texas City proper. It was a very small, shotgun-style house, not much larger than a rented trailer. But to me, it was perfect. I even loved the landscape where refineries loomed, huge and dominant along the horizon—our very own mountain range.

Our dusty yard was enclosed with a broken wire fence, and the sound of freight trains rumbling in the distance felt as comforting as a well-loved parent snoring reassuringly close-by. I played alone out of doors quite a bit, but I don't remember ever feeling lonely. There were plenty of other small houses in the area, but ours always seemed set apart, possibly because I rarely saw any of our neighbors. The highway also was in view, but I mostly ignored it. The flatbeds lumbering by with their loads of pipe for the pipe lines that would connect the Oklahoma oil fields to our mountainous refineries held little interest for me. The only reason I remember them at all is because my father, on his good days, would lift me onto his shoulders and tell me to be proud of the contributions that my very own family was making to the future of our great state of Texas.

He would tell me all about the enormous ship channel that was all built and dedicated in 1914 the very year I was born. He said that it was already connecting our state (and therefore our country) to other shipping ports all over the world. He would tell me this was just the beginning.

"Remember, Gracie, you was here! Right here when it all got started! And your ole Pappy was right durn smack in the middle of it all!"

Then he would describe the enormous barges that labored within the Port of Houston, some as tall as trees, and he promised (in vain, as it turned out) that one day soon, he would bring me there to see it. And he would laugh, and swing me back down to the ground. Then he'd go inside the shanty and start calling for Mama. I guessed he wanted to tell her all about the ship channel, too. But if she was feeling poorly, he'd just end up getting angry and slamming doors. The slamming scared me.

That's why I liked to play outside, with the trains and the flatbeds and our great State of Texas right there with me—even on bad wind days, when the winds shifted from the Gulf, and the nasty, rotten-egg smell of sulfur from the refineries wafted our way.

Though my parents never discussed their personal demons with me, even as a child, I grew to understand that my mother's days of "feeling poorly" and her staying in bed for days at a time were not physical, like consumption or migraines, but emotional. Her suffering seemed to steal a bit more of her after each episode—just like the storm surge stealing bits of the shore when it retreats back out to sea.

I rarely complained, for, my mother was everything to me, and I was loath to displease her. Her dark, wavy hair fell forward on her face, and she had a habit of reaching up to tuck it behind her ear. It never stayed put for more than a few minutes, and so her gesture grew automatic, and she flicked the hair back even if it had not yet tumbled out of place. So familiar was her habit that, later on, I came to understand that the hair falling forward, but left uncorrected, served as a harbinger of an oncoming "episode"—another long, anxious time of waiting for my *real* mother to return.

On her good days, my mother liked to wear knee-length, lightweight "housedresses," as they used to be called. The dresses were airy and spacious, and her white legs and arms poked out like forks stuck into a potato. On her feet she mostly wore sensible sneakers, with no stockings. She also favored an apron during the day because, she told me once, it had enormous pockets. She thought it quite inconvenient that women's clothing tended to use pockets only for decoration if at all, and not for the very useful purpose they served.

Her aprons fascinated me. She used them very well for all manner of things, from holding the duster when she needed her two hands to move things here and there on the shelves as she worked, to collecting small toys like my jacks set that seemed never to leave the floor unless she picked them up, to an enormous store of safety pins that became affixed to the apron itself.

Sometimes, when she was smiling and flipping her hair back throughout the day, and fixing me grilled cheese sandwiches and tomato slices for my lunch, she would let me practice tying bows by working with the two sashes at the back of her apron. Since she favored the style that went over your head, the apron was never in any danger of falling off. I would stand on a vinyl-covered kitchen chair directly behind her as she grilled the sandwiches, my face worked into a serious frown as I struggled to master the very difficult task of creating a bow from two unwilling sashes. When the sandwiches were done, she would laugh, and tell me to go get washed up for lunch. Then she would tie the bow herself with both hands behind her back. This feat fascinated me for years. How could she ever manage that? And her bows were perfectly symmetrical and never lopsided, as the best of mine would inevitably be.

Once, instead of a bow, I managed to tie such a great knot that even my mother couldn't unravel it. We had to wait and have my father help after he returned home from work. He frowned and asked her how she managed to get herself tied up in knots like that. She never did tell him our little secret. Instead, she turned and winked at me as Daddy struggled with the knot, and afterwards, she and I laughed and hugged and then laughed some more while Daddy shrugged, and headed into the living room to listen to the news on our stereo receiver, and wait for his supper.

When my mother took ill, during one of her spells, we sometimes had no supper. Daddy would make peanut butter sandwiches and leave the dirty dishes in the sink, which worried me. Mother always cleaned up right away. Wouldn't she be angry if she came out in the middle of the night and saw the mess? Why wasn't Daddy worried about it, too? I tried to help by pushing the vinyl chair closer and trying to lean in over the sink to do the washing-up myself, but Daddy stopped me. He said not to worry, it would all get done in good time. And I took heart in the hope that he somehow knew that my mother would be feeling better soon.

I don't know what the timeframes were, but, some of my best days were when I awoke to the twangs of country music playing on the radio receiver, or the tub in the tiny bathroom filling with water, or the smell of frying bacon. Any of these, all of them, signified that my mother—my *real* mother—had finally returned! I would leap from my bed and run as fast as I could to be safe in her arms again at last. She would hug me gingerly, as I recall. Almost as though she feared I might break. Or maybe she feared that she might fall apart if she gave herself, too soon, to her world. I don't think it mattered either way.

If my father was around, he would tell me to go play, to leave her be, and give her time to rest and regain her strength. Even I could see that her smile seemed wan and tired, and that she looked even more spindly in her puffy housedress than before. So I would tiptoe around the house for a day or two, or play outside, being careful to stay within earshot in case she called. She rarely did, though. Sometimes, I think she forgot to make lunch until I appeared in the kitchen when the town church bells chimed noon, and seated myself quietly at the table. Those early lunches—made in haste—generally were not her best fare. She would butter thick slices of bread and plop some bologna onto them, pour a glass of milk for me, and then resume her long, languid humming along with whatever sad- sounding song happened to be playing on the radio receiver. A day or two (or three) after that, she would be smiling again, and we would make the rounds during the day, cleaning the house, picking up my jacks, tying apron bows and snuggling on my father's chair in the living room, reading books from the lending library, before he returned home to claim his rightful place.

Those are some of my earliest memories. As I grew a bit older, I began to skirt the surface of our lovely world—to suspect that something about our lives just wasn't quite right. I couldn't put my finger on it; not for a long while. It was as though I had been a tadpole, literally breathing in the water in which we lived and thriving there for a goodly amount of time. But after that, my gills started to close, and I found I was growing lungs. I had to surface more often, and at some point, could no longer live in that earlier world of lovely stillness.

The first thing I remember happening, was, I had to go to school.

One sunny afternoon, as I played outside in the backyard alone during one of my mother's bad days, the woman who owned our home, Mrs. Schultz, came over to collect that month's rent. I'd seen her before, but we had never spoken, as I generally liked to hide in my room when we had visitors (come to think of it, the only visitor I remember, back then, was Mrs. Shultz).

Mrs. Schultz had appeared from around the side of the yard and was standing there in her housedress and wearing a bonnet, due to the late summer heat. She stood there, fanning herself with a newspaper or a folder of some sort, staring at me. I remember that I began to feel distinctly uncomfortable, so I turned away from her and played even harder, scooping the dry dirt into a jar and talking to myself softly all the while. I always talked to myself back then, and made up stories to amuse myself as the hours ticked by.

"Where is your mother?" Mrs. Schultz finally said.

I remember that I shrugged. I didn't like visitors. Neither did my mother.

"Is she in the house, dear?"

Around that time, a freight train rumbled past. I pretended that Mrs. Schultz was the train conductor, and soon she would be whisked off to a faraway land.

"I want to see your mother," Mrs. Schultz said again. Only this time she sounded louder and maybe like she was starting to get angry.

"I've been knocking on the front door for at least ten minutes," the intruder continued. "It was only by chance that I saw you were out here, and thought your mother must be close by. But I don't see her," Mrs. Schultz said again. She was frowning. I could tell by the tone of her voice. I tried to shrink away into nothing so she would go away and leave us alone. How lucky my mother was, to be safe inside!

Suddenly, I had an irresistible urge to go inside and be with my mother, maybe even hide underneath her bed. Completely ignoring Mrs. Schultz, I jumped up and tossed a handful of dirt into her general direction at the same time. Terrified (for I'd never done anything that rude before in my entire six years of life), I ran into the house, clambering up the three porch steps and forgetting to slam the screen door behind me. I screamed for my mother as I ran through the kitchen and down the short hall to where the two bedrooms were, and I pulled on the doorknob, vainly trying to twist it open.

"Mama! Mama!" I remember that I cried. "There's a witch out here! She wants to eat us for supper!"

Now, I have no earthly idea where that idea had come from—probably the fairy tales books from the library that my mother and I would pore over, when she was feeling up to it.

I turned around and was horrified to see Mrs. Shultz standing in the hallway behind me. She seemed so big that she blocked all the daylight from the doors and windows behind her. I must say, that was the closest I'd ever come to fainting, back then.

She approached me in a no-nonsense fashion. I shrank back as far as I possibly could into the corner at the end of the hallway. I was trapped. She ignored my shaking form as she, too, leaned in closer and knocked on the door, calling out for my mother, and then trying the doorknob herself, but it must have been locked. Foiled in her attempts to contact my mother, she returned her attention to me.

"Come here, please," Mrs. Schultz said firmly. She extended her hand. I noticed that she'd taken off her bonnet and gotten rid of the newspaper, or whatever it was she'd been using as a fan when we were outside. I pushed past her and pulled and jiggled the bedroom doorknob again, vainly calling, "Mama! Mama!"

Mrs. Schultz began to speak soothingly, as though I was a frightened little kitten—which, I guess, in a way I was. "Come back into the kitchen, dear," she said. Utterly defeated, I turned and kicked my mother's bedroom door. Then I slowly walked over to Mrs. Schultz, and she took my hand (I still refused to offer it). We went into the kitchen, and she moved her bonnet aside (it was on the kitchen table). Then she held me up over the sink and helped me to wash my face and hands. I still wouldn't look at her, much less, say one word. But she didn't seem to notice.

Instead, she carried me over to the table put me on a chair. (She put me in my mother's spot! My mother always sat in that spot, because it faced the window and she loved to look outside while we had our meals. What a stupid lady Mrs. Shultz was, I told myself. She didn't know anything about us.)

Within a short time, Mrs. Schultz had washed her own hands and then helped herself to our refrigerator. I remember feeling completely incensed and like I wanted to call the police, but I didn't move. Maybe Daddy would be home soon. He would know what to do. He would get rid of her!

Looking back, I guess I had to stay angry in order to keep my absolute terror at bay. And even worse than that—my feeling of betrayal and abandonment by my perfect mother, who should have been out of her bedroom by now and trying to protect me.

Instead, I sat there, not talking, not moving. Mrs. Schultz worked quickly and efficiently. She pulled things from the refrigerator and the pantry, and washed the plates and silverware in the sink. She pulled the old frying pan out of a cabinet and washed it *before* she used it. More evidence (I thought) of her stupidity!

But soon she had served me a cheese omelet and buttered bread, along with a large glass of milk. She sat there while I first stared at my plate, and then couldn't help myself. I was starved, because I hadn't eaten since Daddy made his signature peanut butter sandwiches for our dinner last night. I ate everything she offered. It was all completely delicious. She, herself, ate nothing, which I took to be something finally in her favor. At least she wasn't trying to steal from us. She didn't talk to me, either. Instead, she casually peeled a large red apple, and then cut it into slices. I ate them, every one. Afterwards, I tried to put the dishes in the sink, but she told me that was okay, she would take care of it. She asked me if I had any homework. I remember how her question puzzled me. Homework?

"Sometimes, I help Mama with the dusting," I told her (my first words in the last hours).

"That's very nice, dear. But I'm asking about homework. You know, school work. Don't you go to school? How old are you?"

"Six," I said proudly.

"You should be in first grade," Mrs. Schultz declared. "School began on Monday. You should have been in school for three days, by now. Don't your parents take you to school each day?"

Bewildered, I shook my head. Mrs. Shultz frowned.

"Oh, dear," she said. She reached over and gently inspected my shoulder-length brown hair.

"Ouch!" I cried, and jumped back, my suspicions of her renewed.

She bit her lip. "I may be overstepping," she said, more to herself than to me, I suppose. "But this child is filthy! Her hair is in knots. Come on," she said, this time definitely talking to me. "Let's get you cleaned up."

She led me into the bathroom, and carried along one of the red vinyl-covered chairs from the kitchen.

"Here, dear," she said, not unkindly. "Let's have you kneel on this chair and lean over the sink, so I can help you wash your hair."

She didn't do things nearly as elegantly as my mother, but, by the time Mrs. Schultz was done, my hair was shiny and combed out perfectly. Even I had to smile at myself in the mirror. Then she soaped up a wash rag and got me as clean as she could, without tossing me into the tub.

"Now, one more thing. Where's your toothbrush?"

She scrubbed my teeth herself, which hurt, and which I didn't like one bit. But she seemed pleased by the result, so I felt like maybe that indignity had been worth it, too.

"Do you have children?" I asked her suddenly.

She started. It was the first thing I'd spoken to her voluntarily all afternoon.

"Why, yes, I do, dear. I have three. Two boys and a girl."

"How come you never bring them here to play with me?" Mrs. Schultz laughed.

"My children are grown!" she told me. "They all live far away. But they bring their own families to visit when they can."

"Oh," I told her.

By the time my father returned home from the refinery, Mrs. Schultz and I were great friends. She was playing a reading game with me in which she told me the sounds the letters made and then put two or three letters together so I could sound them out and guess the word. It was great fun, and we were both giggling and didn't even hear Daddy until he was right in front of us. I remember that my heart froze. *We were sitting in his chair!*

"What in the hell do you think you're doing?"

"Daddy!" I cried, and tumbled from the armchair and hurried over for my hug. "I'm sorry, Daddy! I won't sit there anymore!"

But it wasn't my transgression that had caught and held his auger-like gaze. "Not now," Daddy told me. He still hadn't taken his eyes off of Mrs. Schultz.

"You'll get your rent check, ma'am. Soon as I get paid, you'll get your money. You leave my kid alone. Do you hear me? Where's Elaine?" he suddenly asked, looking around for Mama.

"I don't know where Elaine is," Mrs. Schultz said bravely. She stood up and faced my daddy straight on. She was at least a head shorter than he was, but somehow that didn't seem to matter. I saw no fear in her eyes, the way that Mama sometimes looked fearful. Or, looked away. Mrs. Schultz just kept staring back directly at him.

"*You* tell *me* where your wife is, sir," Mrs. Schultz continued. "I came by to ask about the rent, yes, but what I found was this little girl outside, completely unsupervised!"

Daddy cut her short by turning to me and saying, "Gracie, hon, you go on outside and play. Let us grownups have a minute, okay?"

I looked from Daddy to Mrs. Schultz uneasily, but both of them seemed to agree on this course of action.

"Go on outside, dear," Mrs. Schultz encouraged. "But don't you wander off from the porch. Your father is here, so everything will be all right."

Reluctantly, I headed for the screen door. I turned around to look at them again before I went outside, and both of them were standing there, watching me. I felt like slamming the door, or kicking it, or doing something to let them know how mad I felt at being dismissed like that. But I didn't. Something about Daddy's face made me know that this time, for sure, I needed to obey.

So I hid behind the hedge beneath the window just outside the living room. The evening was still very warm, so the window was open and the screen was in place. I could hear everything.

"Who in the hell do you think you are? You can't just bust into my home and act like you own the place!" my father's voice thundered.

"It so happens that I *do* own the place," Mrs. Schultz answered bravely. "And you, sir, cannot allow your six-year-old child to be unsupervised all day! She ought to be in school!"

"Elaine will take care of all that," my father seethed. "Soon as she's feeling more like herself."

"What is going on with your wife, sir?" Mrs. Schultz asked, suddenly calm. "She won't answer her door, and she's locked herself in."

"She's what? She's locked in? Elaine. Elaine! It's me! Open up, you hear me?"

I couldn't see what was going on, but things got so loud that I could well imagine the scene: my father calling as he fairly danced down the short hallway, and then standing at the door jamb, pulling and pushing on the knob, and Mrs. Schultz wringing her hands behind him. I found it both fascinating, and terrifying.

Suddenly I heard a loud, dull *crack!* And Mrs. Schultz was yelling at my father about how he'd broken the door. And my father was yelling at my mother to get up out of the bed and be a real wife, and Mrs. Schultz was demanding to be given a reason not to go call the parish priest—who knew the owner of an orphanage and was at liberty to make a call to him at any time, day or night.

I crawled out from behind the bush, around then. I wanted to go play. I pretended I was a butterfly (my long hair made me feel pretty, now that Mrs. Schultz had put some yellow grosgrain ribbons in it). I was still flitting around the yard some time later (by now, I was vainly trying to capture fireflies in the glass jar I'd found beside the road) when Daddy and Mrs. Schultz both came out of the house.

They even shook hands before she left. I wanted to run over and give her a hug goodbye, but she only nodded to me before she walked around to the front. I heard her car start, and then she drove away.

"Come on inside now, Gracie," Daddy said.

"Time for you to go to sleep. You got school tomorrow."

About the Author

Peggy Stautberg is an information management and documentation specialist for an oil company headquartered in Houston. She also provides line and developmental editing services on a freelance basis to authors of fiction and nonfiction. She is working on her first novel.

Saved by the Bull

By Robert John DeLuca

SAVED BY THE BULL

THE GRIZZLED OLD MAN mindlessly scratched the week-old stubble on his chin as he prattled on to the two people standing on his porch. "I know you folks appreciate how lucky you are to have the privilege of spending some time on the beautiful Sunnyside Ranch. I am very careful who I let come out here. We have the best grazing land in all of Texas to say nothing of the teeming wildlife all over the place," he boasted.

Try as I might it was tough for me to pay strict attention to the never ending nuggets of wisdom that rolled off this gentleman's tongue, mainly because I had heard them all before, many, many times. It was late September and my eight-year-old grandson and I were suffering through our annual lecture from the landowner of several hundred acres of open fields and woodlands in the Hill Country southwest of Austin, Texas. A Houstonian strapped to a desk for my entire working career, I had leased the right to hunt on his property each fall for several years. Unfortunately, in addition to a hefty wad of greenbacks, the price included having to put up with his "laying down the law" about proper deportment while traversing his sacred ground.

Although he could be overbearing as omnipotent king of Sunnyside Ranch, Franklin Dimmer was actually an affable old fellow, once you broke through the veneer of his outward crustiness. Fast approaching eighty, he lived alone in a double-wide some three or four miles from the nearest hard surface pavement along a white dusty caliche lane. Decidedly stooped by his advancing years and a lifetime of physical toil around the ranch, Franklin was still a big man, who must have cut an imposing figure in his heyday. No doubt, his size alone helped him to finagle his will on those around him. With us he used his position as exalted lord of the land to make sure we clearly understood that he was in control.

A bulbous nose dominated his reddened face, which was perhaps the result of the intense southwest sun or, more likely, a clandestine stash of sour mash whiskey. His ruddy complexion accentuated bulging jowls supporting a large mouth that flashed still surprisingly white gleaming teeth. His deep set, dark brown eyes conveyed the sense that he was a serious no-nonsense soul. It took a while, but after you got to know him, those same eyes betrayed frequent flashes of warmth and even amusement, which were more in line with his true personality. Shocks of gray hair squirted out in haphazard places from under a battered ten-gallon hat which he wore at all times. Whenever we walked up to his place we never knew what to expect when Franklin abruptly appeared behind the glass storm door of the double-wide. During the first few years he was always nattily attired in neatly pressed jeans and brightly colored western shirts with braces and highly polished cowboy boots. More recently, since the passing of his precious wife to cancer, he had become more casual in his dress. He was quite a sight in a sleeveless tee shirt, boxers, and, of course, the ten-gallon lid.

I have always looked forward to the fall in the Lone Star state, when the heat finally eased off for a while, and life was more than just dashing from air conditioned space to air conditioned space. It seemed like I spent most of the rest of the year in the Bayou City crawling through paralyzed big city traffic. As a consequence, I have enjoyed being able to escape to the comparative tranquility of the country on ranches such as Franklin's. His place was hardly postcard perfect. In fact, his six to seven hundred acres were cross-fenced with innumerable barb wire mazes, pastures, gates, pens, and work areas. A motley assortment of long abandoned rusted farm equipment and implements were randomly strewn about. The tract was perhaps half wooded with gorgeous stands of thick live oaks, ash, beech, hickory, mulberry, and dozens of other varieties of trees. The open fields were covered with native Texas pasture grasses and frequent clumps of prickly pear cactus, which I have, on several painful occasions, come into close proximity. A rocky intermittent stream bed snaked through the middle of his property. Sometimes there was water and at others it was dry. Franklin had long since given up any effort to work Sunnyside. Other than a few hunters and occasional cattle grazers, we virtually had the place to ourselves.

With a hint of autumn crispness in the air, there are few settings more delightful and soothing than the serene Texas woodlands late in the day as the golden setting sun radiates through the wild foliage. Who needs electronics, computers, iPods, etc.? Mother Nature puts on a show that rivals anything that ever popped out of a cathode ray tube.

Before I give the impression that I am a complete tree hugging freak, I must confess to the "rest of the story". While I absolutely adore the peacefulness of the Texas woods in the autumn, I am admittedly out there for a purpose. As is the case with well over one million other license holders in the state, I am a deer hunter. Through the years this avocation has consistently proven to be a marvelous self-enriching family activity. As the father of four sons, the hunt has for decades now provided us with something several of us can still do together. The tradition has now even trickled down to my grandchildren. Also, as a coronary patient with one heart attack and several stents in my arteries, venison has replaced fatty beef in my diet. Any deer I happen to take ends up on our dinner table. I know, the sinfulness of a Texan rejecting beef is right up here with thinking that Alamo is a rent-a-car company.

I glanced down and noticed that my partner, grandson Bruce, had totally tuned Franklin out and was now avidly swatting and crushing black "love bugs" that swirl around the porch in great numbers. Love bugs are a species of South American fly that suddenly appear in south Texas in the fall during mating season, when pairs of them become stuck together and fly around end-to-end. (I was happy Bruce did not ask me what they were doing.) Franklin finally wound up his "rules and regs," and with a captive audience, he seamlessly slipped into storytelling mode. He launched into the one about the wild cougar on the roof whose tail swooshed by the window when he was at the sink washing dishes. I had to cut him off soon or we would have been out there until Christmas.

"Ah, Franklin. Franklin?" I interrupted, "The cattle. What about the cattle on the ranch? And the bull? Are they still out there?" Franklin had conveniently left this somewhat contentious subject out of his lecture.

The old man stopped mid-sentence, and did his best to conjure up a steely glare. He remained silent for several seconds. Finally, he responded, "Well, you know that the Sunnyside Ranch has some of the best grass in all of Texas that is chock full of nutrients cows thrive on." I gave him a slight nod, which is more than this drivel deserved. "So, with my place in great demand, I could hardly say 'no' when the cattle folks called."

"Oh, I see. Is it the same herd of obnoxious longhorns with that huge bull, Apollo?" I asked.

He looked away and swatted at a love bug himself before grunting something all but unintelligible. I took it as a "yes".

I had expected as much. Many landowners, such as Franklin, who are less than impartial on the matter, argue that cattle grazing and deer hunting are very compatible activities. The wild deer get used to seeing the ponderous bovines stumbling around the fields. Neither is a threat to the other. Even I have observed deer feeding quite placidly in the proximity of a bunch of cows. On the other hand, I can attest to the fact that when the "moo cow monsters" are around we see fewer deer. It only makes sense. The noisy and smelly cows reduce two of the deer's most important safeguards. Successful deer hunting is predicated on quiet and stealth, both of which you can forget when cattle are all around you.

He might have been on the ropes but the old guy wanted to prove he had some fight in him yet. He came right back with both barrels. In fact, the sneaky s.o.b. avoided me entirely, and peered down at young Bruce, who interrupted his fly smashing to look up. With a wide I-just- won-the-calf-roping-competition smile the geezer asked, "Son, do you know that we have real Texas longhorns on this ranch? You know, the cows that have horns longer than a school bus?"

Bruce was nobody's kid sister, and he had heard of longhorns, but the school bus size horns was brand new material. He processed things for a moment and said "Really?"

I was tempted to head this stuff off at the pass, but curiosity got the better of me.

Honestly, if I had to identify something that embodied the most widely held perception of Texas, the longhorn would be at the top of my list. These magnificent beasts are absolutely incredible. When you observe them grazing in an open field as I have done so often, it seems amazing that they can carry on normal daily activities with that magnificent width of pointed bone that extends out from either side of their heads. Yet they are quite adept at reaching grass through fences and never seem to impale each other even in close quarters. The cows have spreads of up to six feet and the steers often a foot wider, although I believe school buses are a little longer.

Franklin now had Bruce's rapt attention and was not about to give up. "Yup, that's a fact.

You should see our bull, Apollo, He is a big one. Do you want me to tell you a little about longhorns?"

Bruce was hooked and quickly nodded that he did

"Apollo and his girlfriends trace their history back some five hundred years to when Spanish settlers with Christopher Columbus brought their first cows over here from Europe. Many more were eventually sent to Mexico and some wandered up the Rio Grande valley not far from here. In the 1700's when our government gave away large land parcels in Texas, ranching became popular. I am sure you know that our longhorns are darned tough. They are very healthy and produce many new calves. Also, they have strong legs that could stand up under long cattle drives, which became common, especially in south Texas."

"Our longhorns became one of the favorite types of cattle in the late 1800's. The longhorn was a dream. You could leave them on their own for most of the year in the scrub country. Then herd them together and drive them to railheads and slaughter houses. Sadly, though, cattle men discovered that other breeds would do even better in closed pens called feedlots. Long drives weren't needed to get them to market. Also, the longhorns never got sick, but sometimes they carried ticks that infested the local cows up north. So, do you know what happened then?"

With wide inquiring eyes, Bruce replied, "No, sir. What?"

"Well, those dumb people up north decided that our Texas longhorns weren't any good any longer so they began slaughtering them to where in the early 1900's they were almost all gone. Lucky for us, a few families saved the few animals left. Apollo came from that small group. We are blessed to have those mighty animals around at all, especially on the Sunnyside Ranch."

Young Bruce was nodding agreeably, but I wasn't buying this woeful, but factual, sob story. Enough was enough. I decided to press Franklin a bit to remind him that at the end of last year's hunting season he promised to give the bovines a boot off his property.

Again, the old guy looked uncomfortable and admitted, "Well, we tried, but it just didn't work out."

What the heck was that supposed to mean? I thought he was lord and master of all he surveyed? The "herd" we are discussing consisted of Apollo, the massive bull, and his personal harem of nine longhorn cows. Needless to say, Apollo was quite partial to his ladies and felt the need to watch out for them. This undisputed king of the pasture was an immense mobile package on four legs, who tipped the scales well over one thousand pounds (half a ton.) His ladies were probably *only* in the eight to nine-hundred-pound range. He stood at least four to five feet at the shoulder and could look me straight in the eye, which he did on several occasions. His hide was mostly a rich dark chocolate brown, although several of the others were mottled and spotted in various shades of brown, white, tan, and gray. There was no mistaking him since unlike his female friends, he had the distinctive thick bull neck. Apollo was a gigantic hunk of animal from stem to stern. Did I mention his horns? Those weapons would not have fit through a normal doorway end on end. They ran out from his head a foot or two, swerved upward, and eventually flared out to sharp points. Many times as I sat there observing him, I imagined the big lug using those things to impale and flip me over a barbed wire fence. He was not designed as a track star, but I was sure with his four-wheel drive he could easily run me down in seconds.

Although Franklin's yarn was historically accurate he had neglected to favor us with some of the more recent developments on his place. Probably because Franklin's grazing rate was too high and not for any other reason, a month or so ago the herd owner had attempted to remove his animals from Sunnyside. It seems that cowboys on horses (And yes, Matilda, we still do actually have real "cowboys" in Texas) had managed to move Apollo to a chute with a ramp into a truck to haul the giant to "greener pastures". Maybe, as Franklin bragged, his grass was so delectable, or for whatever reason, Apollo "put his hoof down", and decided he just wasn't going anywhere. As the wranglers urged him along and up the ramp, the bull suddenly wasn't having any of it. He chose instead to turn around and exit the way he came in. Unfortunately U-turns are discouraged on ramps in very close quarters. There was no room for him to maneuver. To solve his problem, the bull rocked, stomped, and rolled around with tremendous force. The truck rattled and shook back and forth. Something had to give, and it wasn't the four-legged heavyweight. Suddenly, the ramp collapsed and the sides of the chute splintered permitting the unhappy bovine to burst out of jail with violent crash and a shrieking bellow. Once free, he was a freight train steaming back to his harem a few fields away. As if the damaged truck and shattered chute were not enough, in the mayhem one of the cowboys was gored across his arm by flying horns and had to be rushed to a hospital. Apollo could have a bad temper.

While Franklin, had overlooked those events in his remarks, he did make a point to mention that longhorns are known to be "docile and gentle". If I didn't believe him, he could show me a book where it said so. Uh huh.

As I mentioned the hunting season is a usually a time for me to kick back and relax.

Apollo and his women had been out there all last year without incident, except that the deer had disappeared. I'd be darned if I would let Franklin's "bull", one way or another, intrude on my fun. Perhaps Apollo was not the only bull-headed creature out there. Just ask my wife.

***

The first Saturday in November generally marks the opening of whitetail deer season in Texas. As is our custom that day, Allen, my forty-six-year old son, and I were up early and drove out to Sunnyside under cover of darkness. Although, it can get quite nasty, cold, and wet in south Texas later in the season, that day was in the sixties and fair. When we hunt we sit in elevated box stands that are as much as eight to ten feet off the ground. My son headed off through the woods in one direction, and I in the opposite, which, (you knew this was coming) ran right through Apollo's dining room. I was decked out in all my camo hunting garb walking across a muddy field toward a rickety wooden stand a couple hundred yards away. There was nothing but grass and cactus between me and the hunting spot. Well, almost nothing. About halfway out stood our hero and his team spread either side of my path. I could have done an about face and headed back to the truck for some coffee, but I had been a US Marine, hadn't I? We never, almost never, retreat. Also, I was carrying a Ruger 77 .280 rifle, although I hadn't bothered to load it. After all, I had walked past that big tub of lard many times in the past without incident. I hoped he hadn't heard me speak ill of him to Franklin. Undaunted, I resolutely pressed on. As I approached his highness, who was nonchalantly chewing on a large tuft of grass, I caught what seemed to be a very wary look in his beady eyes. *Yeah, I don't like you either.* I swallowed hard but shuffled past him trying to keep my normal pace. I was certain I would soon hear the thundering crash of hooves and a soul-searing bellow as he charged me from behind and pounded me into the mud.

Appreciatively, nothing happened. When I finally reached the stand, climbed the ladder, and sat down, I dared look back at him. The group had moved a little from where they'd been as they do when grazing, but otherwise all looked at peace, although I swear Apollo was smiling at me with his wicked dark eyes.

I tried to put the beast out of my mind and proceed with my hunting, but that turned out to be fruitless. No action. I should have brought a good book. As I had predicted with the cattle company in place, no deer ventured forth. The cows remained out the entire time. I would be lying if the thought of my rifle and those immense targets did not cross my mind, but I did manage to keep some measure of common sense. Of course, Apollo just had to rub it in. I watched helplessly from above as he steadily browsed toward my stand. Then, so as to further irritate me and be darn sure my hunting would be unsuccessful, while almost directly beneath me, he began to swipe his humongous horns along the metal guide wires supporting my perch. I suppose he could have tipped the whole thing over, which didn't happen. What he did do, however, was create a "boing-boing" serenade for anything within a half a mile. Thanks, fat boy!

Huge bulls notwithstanding, our normal hunting routine is to be in place before first light and then get down around 10:00 AM. We relax, have lunch, nap, or watch football until about 3:00 PM when we go back out and sit until sunset. After the wasted morning, I was still hopeful of a more productive second session. As I walked back out to my stand that afternoon, my spirits lifted. Neither Apollo nor his harem were anywhere in sight. Of course, the crew had left plenty of mementos that they had been there. I had to watch my step. I figured the local Luby's Cafeteria had a lunch special in another field, and Apollo had taken his ladies over there. I sure didn't care. Really, no bull.

Unfortunately, the afternoon was also uneventful, and nothing appeared at all. I waited until it was almost dark, and finally gave up.

By the time I climbed down from the stand, it was pitch black. I am always surprised what a vastly different aura the very same woods you have been staring at for hours takes on after the sun goes down. It becomes downright spooky. You just know that every wild creature from miles around is lurking in the shadows. And, oh, my goodness, throw in a coyote howl or two, and you are ready to scramble right back up into the blind and lock the door. No such issues that time, however. As I stomped back alone over the barren field to the truck, my thoughts turned to the scrumptious pot of chicken chili my wife had simmering on the stove and how good a cold beer was going to taste. I was also anxious to hear what animals Allen may have seen. It took fifteen minutes or so for me to approach the truck where my son was already packing up his things.

As I walked up, he gave me a strange look, pointed behind me, and asked, "Say, who's your buddy?"

"Huh?" My head snapped around and not twenty feet away was the thousand-pound hamburger package, calmly watching me while he munched on a big piece of cactus.

"Yikes!"

***

Mid-December and the Christmas season were upon us and my chances of getting a deer that year were becoming increasingly slim. As schedules worked out the only possible hunting companion I had that Saturday turned out to Bruce, my eight-year-old grandson, who was always willing and anxious to go, although still too young to be an actual hunter. Nonetheless, he would be decked out in complete camo gear just like the rest of us real hunters. He was a sandy haired sixty-five-pound bundle of energy, who still retained the wonderful childhood innocence that he was sadly destined to lose in the next few years. We sat together in the stand. It is not normally a good practice to hunt without another adult, especially if you happened to have had health problems in the past. But what the heck. Sunnyside was a fairly tame place, massive, angry bulls notwithstanding. What could happen? In fact, since opening day, I had hardly seen Apollo. Bruce and I would "hunt" for a few hours in the morning, and then head in for lunch. I was pretty sure that, cows or no cows, his chatter and constant barrage of questions would keep us from seeing any deer anyway. I turned out to be right on that score.

We caught a beautiful day in the south Texas Hill Country. The temperature was in the fifties, but it was clear and with hardly a puff of breeze. My chatty Bruce was all eyes and ears, and I thoroughly enjoyed his company. We "hunted" until a little after 9:00 AM, when we both agreed to head in and see what Nana would fix us for lunch. I got up and shoved open the door to the stand which tended to stick at the bottom. For some reason, maybe I thrust a little too hard, the door suddenly flew open. My leaning and pushing had lurched me forward, and I lost my balance. I tried in vain to grab the edge of the door frame as I felt myself tumble head first out of the deer blind from about ten feet up. I don't remember much after that, but I obviously struck the hard ground below with a thud. I guess I was lucky to just miss a sharp metal stake, which had been pounded into the ground to hold a guide wire.

As I lay there, I vaguely remember seeing my hysterical grandson standing over me in tears. I heard him asking if I was all right and pleading for me to get up. At least he had been able to climb down the ladder from the stand on his own. I wanted to answer but could not and then, I guess, I passed out completely. What a fool I had been to take a youngster out there all alone. We were in a fix. Bruce was crying and very upset. He tried his best to wake me up but could not. He had no idea what to do. Franklin's trailer was miles away. I have no idea where my cell phone was. I was bleeding from my mouth and certainly had internal injuries. I needed medical attention right away. No one would miss us for hours. It might be too late.

As I later learned, Bruce sat with tears streaming down his face trying desperately to wake me up, he glanced up and screamed. Standing there right next to the deer stand was the huge longhorn bull Mr. Franklin had told him about. Apollo was bigger even than he had imagined, especially being down right at his level. His horns did go on forever, maybe even wider than a school bus. They sparkled in the bright sunlight. Bruce's first impulse was to run, but there was nowhere to go or hide. Maybe he could climb back up the ladder, but he really didn't want to leave Granddaddy alone with that monster. His rifle! But it was still up in the blind.

Somehow Bruce was able to control himself and hold back his tears. He was about to yell at the beast to go away, when he noticed something funny about the animal's eyes. He told me later, the bull did not look mean, mad, or ready to charge. Instead he looked calm, and almost friendly.

Bruce froze as the huge creature moved slowly forward and placed his massive horns so that part of the left beam actually touched the boy's quivering shoulder. The movement was slow, gentle, and deliberate. He pushed a little harder, and all of a sudden Bruce began to understand: Apollo was trying to get him to move. He slowly got to his feet and took a few steps in the direction he had been pushed. The bull took another step, and Bruce began to walk slowly across the field back toward the truck. As he walked the massive animal patiently followed a few steps behind. After what seemed like forever they reached the truck.

Bruce began to cry again. Being at the truck wouldn't help. He couldn't drive. What good was that? Maybe he should run back to Granddaddy?

Apollo almost seemed to sense his frustration and swung his immense head to look down the road. He took a step toward Bruce, who decided to walk in that direction. Again the bull followed him a few steps behind. It was surely an incredible sight: an enormous thousand pound Texas longhorn gently guiding a tiny youngster down a woodland trail. Twice they came to forks. Bruce glanced at Apollo, who looked in the direction he wanted him to go. They covered most of a mile before Bruce told me later that he rounded a bend and saw a red pickup truck with a man in the bed pushing hay bales out for the rest of Apollo's harem that was surrounding the truck in a semi- circle. His heart leapt, and he ran toward the truck shouting.

"Mister! Mister! It's my Granddaddy. He's hurt bad. We need to go to him."

The man in the truck, who happened to have a large bandage on one arm, looked up and saw a young boy in hunter's camo frantically coming toward him.

"Where is he? What happened? Get in. Let's go find him." The man helped the boy up into the cab and jumped into the driver's side. The truck roared off back toward where I lay unconscious. The big bull was nowhere to be seen. He had melted off into the brush.

As it turned out Apollo just might have saved my life. Besides a badly fractured leg, I had suffered internal injuries which caused excessive bleeding. The truck driver immediately called 911 and within a half hour a Life Flight copter from the Stone Oak Hospital in San Antonio settled down in the field right next to the deer stand. I was swooped away and hustled right into surgery at the hospital. Christmas and New Year's weren't much that year but after just a few months I was almost back to normal.

During my hospital stay I was pleasantly surprised one afternoon, when, who popped into my room, but Mr. Franklin Dimmer, himself. He even brought me a bouquet of drooping dandelions straight from the Sunnyside Ranch. He appeared as the old Franklin complete with a western shirt, pressed jeans, and polished boots. He even carried his hat. We were surprised to see that he still had a full head of fluffy hair.

Franklin doesn't mince words when he has something important on his mind, for which I was grateful. I was *really* a captive audience at that point, had he gone into his story mode, cougar tails and all.

"Look", he began, "You were dead right. Those cows and that bull have got to go. I am working on that right now."

Apparently feeling he had finally told me what I wanted to hear, a perplexed look appeared on his face when I replied, "No, Franklin. Let them stay. I have no beef with Apollo. Longhorns are very intelligent animals. I know it says it in a book somewhere, or maybe on the internet."

About the Author

As a businessman **Robert John DeLuca** was compelled to operate within tightly restrictive parameters defined by market conditions, government regulations, and other restraining variables. As an author he enjoys the incredible freedom limited only by his own creativity and passion. He has always had a strong interest in writing, which he cultivated at Brown University and the University of Pittsburgh, where he earned BA and MBA degrees respectively.

After serving as a Captain with the United States Marine Corps in Vietnam he joined the Mellon Bank in Pittsburgh, where he was a national accounts lending officer. Eventually, he settled in Houston as the CFO of a residential construction company. He was also a lender with the local office of Citibank, N.A and became a partner in a shopping center development company. He subsequently founded Desert Southwest Realty. More recently, he developed affordable housing using tax credits. In fact, his extensive business background provides a strong platform and fertile resource in support of his writing endeavors

He has published two books: ***The Pact with the Devil***, a novel pitting a head-strong Texas entrepreneur against a vicious Mexican drug lord and, ***The Perfect Pro Football Coach***, a non-fiction work ranking every NFL head coach over the past fifty years. A second and sequel novel, ***The Master of Deception*** in which a cunning manipulator embezzles millions from several government agencies, will be published this spring. A memoir, ***Beatles, Books, Bombs, and Beyond,*** set in the turbulent 1960's, which is a self-account of life as an ROTC student on an ultra-liberal Ivy League campus and a tribute to fallen Marine Vietnam comrades, will also be published this year. He won first place in the Texas Authors, Inc. Short Story Contest in 2016. His website: **http://bobdelucaauthor.com/**.

A New Englander by birth and jarhead by choice, Mr. DeLuca left Boston before the Patriots stopped being a joke. He has raised a family of four sons, and resides with his awesome wife, grandchild-of-the-week, and bullmastiff in Friendswood, Texas.

THE LITTLE THINGS

By David Welling

THE LITTLE THINGS

FAMOUS LAST WORDS: "I can make it to the next gas station."

With the first cough of the engine, Joel realized his folly. In an almost—but not quite—comical fashion, he tried to nurse their SUV as far as possible. He gained a few hundred yards before the car rolled to a stop along the side of the road, well past the last town, and not a building in sight—hardly an ideal place to be on Christmas Eve.

Joel's reaction came off as neither parentally responsible nor festive, letting forth a series of expletives normally shielded from his son, Paulie.

"Dad, you're not supposed to talk like that," the boy said.

In the passenger seat, Melinda simply glared. She didn't have to say a thing. They had already covered the subject earlier when he passed the first station. "It's on the other side of the highway," he'd answered. "Anyway, I can still get another fifteen miles after I hit E." So he drove past the station, figuring he had plenty of time, followed by another station five miles further down the road, and another after that. Then they exited the highway, gas forgotten—until now.

Joel spent the next few minutes evaluating the situation, mapping out a strategy, and considering options, which were few. For months, Melinda had badgered him to join AAA, and he took the path of optimum procrastination. Now regret swept in, as once more, she proved herself right.

At length, she spoke, softly and with more than a trace of irritation. "We're going to be late." This translated as shorthand for a) Why weren't you paying attention, since you need to be the responsible one? b) This wouldn't have happened if we were going to see *your* family, c) You've royally screwed up Christmas, and I'm damned angry with you, but I won't say it.

The way Joel figured, they'd lost themselves in idle conversation as he drove, so she should accept some small portion of the responsibility for his distraction. He tapped his fingers against the steering wheel. "I'm going to find a service station."

"Where? There's nothing around here."

"I saw a sign for the next town a few miles back. It shouldn't be too far away."

Melinda folded her arms. "I'm not walking that distance."

"I didn't ask you to. You stay here. Paulie and I are going."

"Da-a-ad," Paulie whined, drawing out the vowel through his nose.

Melinda shook her head. "The boy doesn't need to go." "No, he's going," countered Joel. "I might need some help. You'll be fine here. Anyway, we always talk about him not getting enough exercise. Case closed"

"I don't want to be left alone. It's dark."

"If we had left Tulsa earlier, like I wanted, we'd be in Todd Mission by now. It's an eight-hour drive without traffic. We could have gotten up early, had lunch in Dallas, and reached your brother's place by evening."

She crossed her arms, her ire matching his. "But we didn't. Now you've stranded us."

"So you gonna walk to the next town with me?" he snapped back.

"No."

He took in a deep, calming breath, let it out. "Mel, you'll be safe here," he said, placing his hand on hers. "Keep the doors locked. You have your cell phone and I have mine, in case you need me."

Joel had no overriding reason to take Paulie. True, the boy spent way too much of his free time in front of the television. Nor would he be of any help. If anything, he'd slow Joel down. No, the reason had to do with mutual suffering. Joel may have created their current problem, but he refused to endure the consequences alone. Lucky Paulie. For the moment, the spirit of Christmas generosity eluded Joel's judgment.

They took to the road. Within minutes, their car faded into the darkness, while before them, the road stretched into an equally rich, deep black.

"Daddy, how far do we need to go?"

"I don't know. Just keep walking."

He should have known the inevitable repeat, which came five minutes later—or four.

Possibly even three.

"How much farther, Daddy?"

"Paulie, we'll get there when we get there." His response spilled out as sour wassail void of holiday cheer.

"But my legs are tired. Can we stop for a minute?"

"No."

"But Dad, I'm really—"

"I said no."

That put a lid on the conversation. Paulie should know better when his dad's upset.

Joel had every right to be pissed, mostly at himself for not paying attention. Now he reaped the consequences in the middle of a deserted Texas nowhere. He'd not seen a single car pass by since they took to foot, in itself unusual. Even the county roads had occasional traffic. The thought further sunk his mood.

A sign came into view, marking the distance to the next town: one mile. All things considered, their predicament could have been far worse—five miles, ten, fifteen. Once there, they could warm up a bit, while Paulie rested his feet. Most importantly, he could buy the necessary can of gas. If Lady Luck decided to be extra generous, they might even find a ride back to their car.

A mile and a quarter perhaps, not too bad.

Except for two things. First, they had the cold to deal with, a point that Paulie kept bringing up. In truth, the temperature fell somewhere in the upper-forties, but the associated wind made it worse. Joel's bigger concern had to do with a pointless trip. Not a single light could be seen ahead, leading him to an unpleasant conclusion of a town zipped tight for Christmas Eve.

This might be another bad call on Joel's part, not a new thing. He was well used to them, not that bad calls made his life easier. He'd often wondered about the joke of a rain cloud hovering over his head. For some reason, he managed to invite life's small unpleasantries on a regular basis. Tonight fell into place as another in a long line.

"Dad, I'm cold."

"Right." Joel stopped and took off his jacket. Paulie eagerly accepted the extra layer of clothing. "Is that better?"

"Yes, Dad. Thanks."

Joel now earned the right to feel the chill, so he walked all the faster. Big legs can do that in a way small legs can't.

"Dad, slow down."

Right. He eased the pace to Paulie's speed, and rubbed his arms to generate some warmth.

Looking ahead, he saw a light for the first time, there on the left side of the road. He hadn't seen it before. Regardless, there appeared to be at least one lit building in town.

"Dad?"

He looked back to see his son further back than before, now looking up to the sky. "Let's go, Paulie."

The boy pointed toward the night sky. "Dad, is that the star?"

"What star?"

"You know, the Christmas star. The one the smart men followed."

"Wise men," Joel corrected.

"Right. Wise men. Is that the one?"

Joel took a moment to look to the sky, letting his eyes adjust to the points of light overhead.

He got to his knees, pulling Paulie closer. "No, that's Mars, the red planet. That's where Martians come from."

Paulie responded with the 'don't BS me' attitude that kids learn all too soon, when the initial mysteries of the world resolve, and new ones arise in their place. "Dad, there are no such things as Martians."

"How do you know?" Joel grinned. "There could be a UFO with little green men zipping above our heads right now. Maybe they're Santa's helpers."

"I'm serious. Which star is it?"

He took a minute to look over the sky before giving up. "I'm not sure, Paulie. Maybe your Mommy would know. We'll ask her when we get back, okay?"

"Okay."

They resumed their pace, now with a lit destination in sight. As one footstep led to the next, Joel considered how they came to this point. Melinda's brother generously invited them to stay over for the holidays, which she immediately accepted. The siblings hardly saw one another now that their parents had died, and knowing this, Joel agreed. He waited too long to get plane tickets, so travel by car made the most sense, even with the distance from Oklahoma. Her brother lived in Todd Mission, just north of Houston, meaning they would spend most of the day in the car.

Had they left early, they might have enjoyed a leisurely Christmas Eve with her family. Instead, they left at noon.

Joel checked his watch: nine seventeen. Even in the best scenario, it would be another hour before they got the car on the road again. The remaining distance diminished—not quickly, but with a slow consistency.

The light ahead revealed an aged gas station, one preserved straight out of the fifties when attendants in uniform pumped the gas and checked the oil as part of standard service. It wore well the passage of years, from the sign positioned near the roadway, to the two pumps themselves, void of credit card slots and touch-screens, and likely of the same age as the station. He figured them to be for decoration, not function.

A lone exterior light on the side of the building, flickered on and off, indicating its weariness to the dark.

As they drew nearer, Joel realized his accuracy: the town appeared to be locked up for the night. Even this one building might be closed; the lights to the sign and above the pumps were off, and only as they drew nearer did he see an interior light to the building—along with movement inside.

"Thankyouthankyouthankyou," Joel said softly for the small miracle.

They crossed the lot, a finish line of sorts, but without the ceremonial ribbon to break through or any cheering crowds. Positioned in the station window, through glass that might not have been cleaned in years too numerous to count, hung an OPEN sign, with handwriting below which read: WELCOME Y'ALL.

Joel opened the door, and a gust of warmth hit them both in the face. The interior of the station appeared much like the exterior, vintage in design, and showing an abundance of wear. Dust settled in every corner. The related smell inside, a mixture of oil and age, reeled in the events of a thousand yesterdays. Behind the counter sat a man who matched the years of the building around him, arms crossed and legs propped up on a nearby stool. He eyed them both with mild interest.

Joel broke the silence. "You open?"

At this, the man gave up a grin that displayed an absence of dental care, teeth darkened and at odds with one another. For what the man lacked in appearance, the sparkle of his eyes compensated in full. "Was last time I checked," he said, voice coarse, but friendly enough. "What can I do you for?"

"We ran out of gas up the road. Looks like the rest of the town is closed for the night."

"I reckon it is, except for me. Folks here are with family." The man paused for effect, and added, "It's Christmas Eve, you know."

Behind Joel, Paulie wandered the narrow aisles, between metal racks filled with potato chips, peanuts, and other snacks. His small footsteps echoed in the stillness.

"So—out of gas, eh?" the man said once more, now setting his feet on the ground. "Heck of night to get stuck. Too bad. We're out of gas here, too."

The man stared at Joel's reaction, one of abject misery, then let forth a roughened cackle. "Just kidding. Yeah, we got gas." His chuckle ended with a loud snort, followed by a sigh. "That's why I'm here. Gotta peddle the petrol to those in need."

Joel feigned an unconvincing laugh. "Do you have any gas cans here?"

The man sniffed and pointed to the rear of the store. "Back wall, bottom shelf, nine ninety-nine plus tax."

As directed, Joel found a metal three-gallon can on the shelf. Judging by the layer of dust on the top, it had occupied that spot for years. He brought it to the counter and pulled out his wallet.

"That'll be ten seventy-eight, plus the gas, of course," the man said, while ringing it up on a register of the same vintage as the building. It let out a *ca-ching* as the drawer popped out.

Joel cast a glance toward the entrance. "What about the pumps. They look sort of... out of date."

"Now don'cha judge a book by its cover. They never failed me yet." He sniffed again before running his index finger across his moistened nose. "By the way, the name's Elmer. Glad to be of help." He extended his hand, fortunately not the one used as a tissue moments earlier.

Appropriate name, Joel thought, shaking the man's hand, while picturing the cartoon character and rabbit hunting. "I'm glad you're open. I don't know what I would have done otherwise."

"How far up the road are ya?"

"About a mile and a quarter. My wife's waiting on us."

At this, Elmer made a soft sound of reproach. "Shouldn't be leaving the lady all by herself, even on Christmas Eve."

Joel slapped a handful of dollar bills on the counter. "I didn't have much choice now, did I?"

"Now, now, didn't mean to get you all in a tizzy. She'll be fine. Ya got far to go once there's gas in the car?"

"Just past the next town. We've got family there."

"That's what it's all about. Family. Friends. It's the time for taking stock of the little things, ya know what I mean?" Elmer handed back a few coins. "You should expect the unexpected on nights like tonight. How come you run outta gas?"

Joel paused, not expecting the directness of the question. "Because I didn't stop at the last station."

"Because?" Elmer's eyed twinkled.

"Because I forgot?"

"Because?"

"I didn't pay attention. Happy?" Joel snapped.

"Ahh," Elmer replied, stretching out the sound as one on knowing. "Ya gotta slow down. Smell the roses. We get so caught up in where we're going, we don't think about where we are, or more important, them folks around us."

"You a preacher or something?"

Elmer offered up another toothy grin. "Nah. Jes' dime- store advice from an old geezer."

"Oh, cool!" came a voice from the rear. "Dad, check this out!"

Joel turned to see Paulie nearby, standing in complete rapture. The object of his attention rested on top of the ice machine. A bright yellow toy dump truck, a big one by adult standards and gargantuan to the eyes of a child, loomed above Paulie like the Holy Grail with wheels—or as Elmer might describe it, "the cat's meow." No mere plastic cheapo, the truck stretched nearly two feet in length, solid metal, moving parts, doors that opened, and battery-operated headlights (with the batteries actually included, so written on the cardboard packaging).

"Dad, can I have that? I really want it, really, really bad!"

Parental Pavlovian conditioning kicked in, and Joel nearly uttered the standard response—No—given that wherever they went, be it grocery store, pharmacy, or any retail, the inevitable "I want this" line arose. Then he paused, opting instead for a more effective answer.

"Paulie, why don't we wait? It's Christmas and Santa will be bringing a bunch of toys."

"But Da-a-ad."

"I know. You remember what Mommy and I have told you about patience? Anyway, we would have to carry it all the way back to the car."

"I can do it, Dad. Please, please, please. I will be extra good today, tomorrow too, and I can use the truck to clean my room, and put all my things in its back, and move them, and, and, oh, please!"

Ahead of Joel lay two futures, one including the truck and one without. He stared at his boy, who now exhibited the classic wide-eyed wistfulness of a sad-faced orphan painting. He knew the outcome that accompanied choice A. For all his enthusiasm, Paulie might carry the truck for a block, two max, before complaining of it being too heavy, and leaving Joel to drag it, along with a full three-gallon gas can for the remaining distance. The alternative, the future sans truck, transformed Paulie into miniature zombie, slumped shoulders, dragging feet—and walking dejectedly slow for the entire distance back. This alternative would stretch the return trip to twice the time.

Joel saw this as a no-brainer.

"Alright, s on, we can get it." At this, Paulie's face lit up brighter than any of the decorated houses they had passed on the trip down from Tulsa. "Are you sure you can carry it back?"

"Oh, yes! Thanks!"

"Ya done good," said Elmer as Joel placed the oversized truck on the counter. "Mark my words... No matter what he gets for Christmas, this here truck's gonna be his favorite."

Joel pulled his wallet out once more. "So what do I owe you?"

Elmer eyed the truck, then leaned back into his chair. "Take it."

"Uh... I can't do that. Let me pay you for it."

Elmer looked Joel squarely in the eyes. "Listen here. I saw the look on that boy's face. That there truck's as much my property as the man in the moon's. It belongs to him, always has. It was simply waiting for him to stop by and pick it up. So consider this a Christmas gift and think no more of it."

Reluctantly, Joel agreed and handed the truck to his son, who in turn struggled with the weight. "You got it, Paulie?"

The boy nodded.

"This is awfully kind of you," Joel said as he picked up the gas can.

"It's the little things, you know what I'm sayin'? Makes life worth living. Not a day goes by where I don't think about it." Elmer studied the boy, then added, "Ya got a ways to go. If you like, I can hold the truck for you until you gas up the car. Come back by and I'll have it waiting for you."

Joel let out a sigh of relief. "That's great. It's a long walk."
"Do I have to leave it?" Paulie worked his best pout.

Joel got to his knees, hands resting on his son's shoulders. "I know you're excited, but we need to get to the car first. I promise, we will come straight back here for your truck. Deal?"

"Deal." The answer came with little enthusiasm. He turned and held the truck out to Elmer. "Thank you, mister."

Elmer showcased his row of snagly teeth. "You're very welcome. You and your family have a merry Christmas."

Joel carried the can outside to the aged pump, accompanied by Paulie, and examined the relic. He lifted the nozzle, expecting it to cough air or remain dormant—but true to Elmer's word, gas flowed into the can without a problem. Soon enough, the two began their trek back to the car. Paulie kept casting glances to the station behind him, its lights getting smaller the further they walked.

The return journey played out differently from the first. Joel's disposition improved, having the gas can in hand. Despite the cold, he enjoyed the walk, taking in the quiet of the surroundings. Trees rustled as the wind swept past leaves and branches, this being the only sound, aside from the steady crunch, crunch, crunch of feet against gravel. Silent night, indeed.

And for the first time this evening, he paid closer attention to the night sky. True, he looked it over earlier when trying to find Paulie's star, but now, *now*, the macrocosm spread out before him, each light a separate beacon. Such a simple thing to take for granted, this tapestry. In the city, stars vanished, washed out by the metropolitan lights; out here, their luminescence held dominion.

They made better time on the return trip, helped by Paulie's brisk step. Joel understood his motivation: the sooner they reached the car, the quicker they'd return to the station and his new truck. At length, the faint outline of their SUV appeared in the distance. Paulie increased his pace as they grew near, and in the last few dozen yards, broke into a run.

"Mommy, Mommy, wait until I tell you!" he shouted before she had time to open the door. He leapt inside, telling her all the minute details of their adventure, and of the truck that awaited him on their return. Melinda looked from Paulie to Joel, who remained outside with can in hand; her raised eyebrow suggesting, *as if all the wrapped presents in back aren't enough?* Joel offered her a smile, then stepped to the rear of the car, feeding gas to a bone-dry tank.

Starting the engine proved to be a momentary challenge. Dry heaves and sputters ensued before the gas flowed freely through automotive veins, engine running.

"Yay!" Paulie cheered, arms raised, as they pulled to the road. "How long 'till we get there?"

"Hours," Joel teased. "Two or three, at least."

The boy knew better. Still, Joel figured that the mile-plus drive would stretch out far longer in the boy's mind than the entire time spent on foot.

As they drew nearer to town, Joel failed to see any lights. A block short of the station, and with no light still apparent, he realized that Elmer might have shut down for the night. After all, this was Christmas Eve. In the final block, the station came into view, lights off. He pulled into the station lot. "Wait here," he said, and stepped out of the car.

"Does Daddy have it?" he heard Paulie ask through the window he had cranked down. Of course, the boy had limited visibility from his vantage point in the rear.

A minute later, Joel opened the back door. "Here's your truck," he said, setting the toy on the seat alongside the boy before getting back in the front. Once more, wheels took to motion, and the SUV sped on to their Christmas destination, leaving the station far behind.

Paulie gave rapt attention to his monster truck, making little "vroom, vroom" sounds and repeatedly switching the headlights on and off, on and off. The strobe light effect transformed the interior into a miniature disco.

Melinda leaned toward Joel, speaking softly. "I can tell him to stop if it distracts you."

He shook his head. "I'm okay."

"Joel," said Melinda after a few more miles had passed in an uncomfortable silence, "There is something about this I don't quite understand."

He kept his eyes glued to the road before him. "Can we talk about it later?"

The weary travelers came at last to their destination, welcomed with the warmest of hugs, the comfort of family, food kept warm in the oven, a comfortable fire to sit by, and wine to take the edge from the day. Paulie wasted no time in showing off the truck to his cousins.

Due to the lateness of the hour, the evening ended all too soon. Melinda put Paulie to bed, his truck resting nearby, and he fell asleep within minutes, to dream of the next morning, Christmas Day, and all its surprises. Joel and Melinda soon nestled under the sheets in their own guest room bed, listening to all the little sounds of the house. "Hon," she said at length, "what about the truck? You never told me."

"What's to tell. The guy closed for the night and left the toy for us next to the gas pump."

"But the station. It looked..."

"I know how it looked."

Melinda said nothing else, pulled the sheets tighter, and angled her body against him. Joel stared at the ceiling, his mind replaying the events of the evening, and the return trip to the gas station. Melinda had every right to question its appearance; the building they returned to looked abandoned: windows broken and partially boarded, a side wall and portions of the roof charred with black from a fire long before, signs askew or missing, and the whole place unkempt, covered with the dirt of neglect. No telling how long the structure had been abandoned. Joel had stepped closer to look inside, but could only see darkness. He told himself that he returned to the wrong place. There must be another station down the road—except for the evidence. Before him, on a crumbled cement slab near one of the broken pumps, rested the toy dump truck. It stood out in its sparkling newness against the age of its surroundings, awaiting the playfulness of a young boy.

Joel moved closer to his wife, bed sheets rustling softly. "Mel, I'm sorry... about earlier tonight. I shouldn't have taken it out on you and Paulie. I'm a jerk sometimes." She gave no response. When he looked over to her, he saw that she had already fallen asleep. Too bad—she would have relished the *'I told you so'* moment. His mind returned to the boy's truck, the hows and whys, but no, he had no way to explain the unexplainable. Then, when logic exhausted itself, he considered the lesser details of the evening—which gave him pause, those moments in time, as well as the numerous transgressions in his own life. It all came down to that, not the great acts but the little things, words spoken kindly or not so kindly, actions with intent for good or ill, a thousand variables that made life worth living.

Pulling himself closer to Melinda, he drifted off, warm against her in the cold winter's night.

About the Author

David Welling is a Houston-based writer, artist, and graphic designer. His lifelong interest in movies (and the places that show them) led to the writing of *Cinema Houston: From Nickelodeon to Megaplex*, which chronicles the history of movie theatres in Texas' largest city. *Cinema Houston* is the recipient of the 2008 Julia Ideson Award from the Friends of the Texas Room, and the Society of Architectural Historians' 2009 Antoinette Forrester Downing Award. He now writes fiction.

His website and blog is davidwelling.com.

Mezclado

By Elizabeth Uresti Domino

MEZCLADO

She stares back at me and all I see beneath the pale spotted alabaster
Tucked behind the strands of burnt umber
Mother

He stares back at me and all I see within the endless ebony pools
Drowning against the sun kissed cocoa
Father

The taunts, the fingers pointing, the whispers of disgust
Boldly and crudely shouted at the market
She ignores

The slammed doors, the hisses of hate, the threat of a baseball bat
Slurs thrown wildly on the street
He ignores

Their laughs as they shove the pants and sweatshirt in the shower
Scorching calls of 'beaner' and 'spic'
I weep

Little chairs, loudly fragmented English, teacher-parent conferences
Educated assumptions based on ignorance
I question

MEZCLADO

The rejection, their fear and distrust of someone
Not one of them, not a native word spoken
I stumble

Pressed against the glass, outside gazing inward
Faster on its axis, spinning, spinning
I am lost

Fragmented pieces of a puzzle, mismatched and worn
Beautifully reflected in the mirror
I am found

She stares back at me and I drown in her abyss
The infinite possibility of who she becomes versus what she is
Daughter

About the Author

Born and raised in Bryan, Texas, she is probably the only Mexican who doesn't know how to speak Spanish. A transplant to Houston, she fell in love with this city, the pulse and have never left. On the verge of a middle age roller coaster with the Husband #2 and their three awkward pubescent teens and one 7-year-old who may or may not be a genius or sociopath along for the ride, she is anything but a grown-up. From baking cupcakes and cutting crusts on PB&J's to late night Depeche Mode concerts and mosh pits, she is a dichotomy.

This leg of her journey began while she was attending the University of Houston-Downtown. After enrolling in a Creative Writing class in Fall of 2007 with a Dr. Joe Aimone for the sake of fulfilling a requisite for an English credit for her art degree, she found that he opened her heart and mind to writing. And ultimately herself. She became addicted to writing, writing workshops and critique groups and in the spring of 2009 contributed four short stories to the on campus publication of *The Bayou Review.* Upon "leaving school," otherwise known as dropping out, she maintained her writing of short stories as well as an online blog entitled Ramblings of an Ovary and then became a staff writer to a lifestyle magazine, *Act Badd*, in 2012 until January of 2014. She also contributed short story fiction and poetry to another blog, Curators of Dopeness from 2014 until early 2016, and was past Vice President and Press Director for the Houston Writers Guild. She was a cast member in the final South East Texas production of *Listen To Your Mother*, a national award winning spoken-word performance. Today she is acting Press Director for Houston Writers House while still managing to maintain the grind of her legitimate 9-5 job that keeps her children fed and her lights on, water running and student loan debt low. Or lower.

Connect with Elizabeth:

Instagram: @browneyedomino
Twitter: @browneyedomino
Blogspot: ramblingsofanovary.blogspot.com

About Houston Writers House

The goals of this organization are to facilitate those in the writing community to network and connect with others to achieve their publishing and marketing goals.

We are dedicated to helping writers improve their craft, build their brand, pinpoint their audience, and improve marketing skills. We support our authors, whether traditionally published or self-published, through critique groups, monthly socials, workshops and conferences providing varying topics from esteemed literary professionals.

Learn more at www.houstonwritershouse.net

www.ingramcontent.com/pod-product-compliance
Lightning Source LLC
Chambersburg PA
CBHW030534310726
48979CB00010B/1900/J

* 9 7 8 0 9 9 1 1 4 3 5 3 5 *